WAVES BREAKING OVER YS

MATT LARKIN

INCANDESCENT PHOENIX BOOKS

Waves Breaking Over Ys
Tales of Dark Faerie Book 1
MATT LARKIN
Editors: Sarah Chorn, Regina Dowling
Cover: Nada Orlic
Map: Francesca Baerald

Copyright © 2023 Matt Larkin.

This is a work of fiction. Names, characters, organizations, places, events and incidents either are the product of the author's imagination or are used fictitiously.
All rights reserved, including the right to reproduce this book, or portions thereof, in any form.

Incandescent Phoenix Books
mattlarkinbooks.com

GOLGLETH
NORTH SEA
FROZEN TUNDRA
CROWN PEAKS
SGITHEANACH
ENCHANTED FOREST
CANTREF GWAELOD
CORRYVRECKAN
THE ALBIA
HINTERLANDS OF FALIAS
DÙN CRUINN
FALIAS
DÙN BEINN
NEMEDIA
INIS FÀIL
STARFALL VALE
KÈR-YS
THE DANU
MYNYDD Y GAER
BRO ERECH
LAKENWALD
THE RENOS
BLACK FOREST
ALBERU
THE SPEAR
OGREPEAKS
INNER SEA
SERPENT COAST
PONTUS
N
W E
BLEAKWOODS

THE WHISPER

It starts with a whisper, a haunting intimation of a World askew. That we are, in the end, caught in a death spiral, time nearly played out, whilst entropy tugs ever harder upon the Wheel of Fate.

Looking now into the dying embers, we at last apprehend Truth, and in it the revelation that the vaunted tales of old were not what we thought ... And neither, in fact, were we.

For if we have lived before, might not all we've dreamt be but our souls' memories of Worlds become dust ...

A QUICK NOTE

For full colour, higher-res maps, character lists, location overviews, and glossaries, check out the bonus resources here:

https://tinyurl.com/432fzhya

If you liked this book, be sure to check out my offer for free books at the end.

PROLOGUE: DAHUT

Washed after her journey—cleansed of that man's touch on her body—Dahut dressed in a fine gown, green as hills in spring. By the time she had finished her ablutions, eventide had begun to creep in and the feast would be underway. Her father, though still weighed by grief over the loss of his wife and son, declared a grand celebration in honour of the return of the young princess, Dahut's sister. The feast would culminate with a naming ceremony. At last they would move beyond the tragedy Bro Érech's king had visited upon Kêr-Ys. On her return, Father did not speak of the accusations Dahut cast upon him when she had left, how she claimed, had Gwezenneg not already thought him a weak king from a failing line, he would not have dared to ambush the queen whilst she visited her kin in the Black Forest. He did not mention how Dahut had named him craven when he refused to march the army against his rebellious subject king.

In fact, Gralon had little to say to her save a weeping embrace of gratitude. Dahut needed to apologise for her bitter words, but before that, she needed rather a lot of wine to help her wash down her pride. She was a druid as well as a princess, and neither druids nor royals were wont to offer apologies. Pride was not always a failing. A woman needed pride to stand against the tribulations of Fate. Pride kept her head high when all the World sought to bow it. She had already shed more of her pride than she could bear.

Dahut sighed, hugged herself. It had taken much to save her sister. Her plan had forced her to seduce Gwezenneg—and to take aid from an Other to do so—who had not known her, and to allow herself to become his consort. Only then had she been able to slay him, recover her infant sister he had stolen, and make her escape from Bro Érech. Only after letting him dirty her flesh with his touch. Some things one could not cleanse with mere washing, for they left stains upon the soul.

She would not show it, though. Not to her father, not to the courtiers filling the grand hall in the palace, not, if she could help it, even to herself. Instead, she knelt at the chest where she kept her clothes and shoved them aside to reveal the iron key hidden beneath. A thin silver chain threaded through the top of it, for Dahut had always worn the key between her breasts, close to her heart. It opened the vault of Kêr-Ys, the legacy of the Smith Lord who had raised this city, hers by right as princess. According to druidic lore, the demigod Gofannon had crafted the city and its walls with the power of the Celestial Jewel that now slept within the palace vaults. Through their father, King Gralon, Dahut and her sister carried the last of Gofannon's divine blood and his greater legacy.

And that wretch Gwezenneg had thought to challenge the might of Ys by murdering Dahut's mother and her brother and trying to hold the infant princess hostage. Father had done naught, wallowing in his mourning, terrified of his daughter coming to harm if he should act. As if abduction was not harm enough. Dahut had refused to wait. Now, the princess was coming home and her abductor, King Gwezenneg, was sped off to the Otherworld, may the fear gorta feast upon his unworthy soul.

Dahut had dared not carry the key to the vault to Bro Érech, where the spectre of death had hovered so nigh to her. Now though, with him dead, with her safe behind the towering granite walls of Kêr-Ys, she donned it once more, tucking it inside her dress. The wall was not the only defence Gofannon had prepared for his creation. At high tide, these gates would be sealed and the isthmus would flood. It made assailing Kêr-Ys impossible, for an army would have but hours to over-come the granite walls—manned by slingers—and the soldiers warding the gates. King Gwezenneg would never have dared strike at the city, but it had not stopped the pompous subject king from breaking his oath of loyalty.

Words, she found, were not worth what they had been.

Much though she might rather have tarried in her chambers, gotten drunk—uproariously so—and passed out, she could ill afford to miss her sister's feast. Thus, like her dress, she donned a smile and made her way downstairs.

IN A CORNER OF THE PALACE, away from the main feast, in a chamber bedecked with fading tapestries, she clanked her goblet against Sétanta's. The young Ysian knight was already flush with more than one cup, but what did it matter? Feasts were for drinking and revelry and making good memories. They sat at a low table, the only people in the room save for a servant trying to blend in with an alcove in the wall, like one of the marble statues of Dahut's ancestors. Light spilled from a lamp on the table, casting flowing shadows over her decanter of wine. This room was closed to the party; not closed for the princess, though.

The knight sat close enough Dahut could smell the musk of his sweat, a scent mingling with the wine and the aroma of roasting pork wafting through the palace. He and his comrade Moccus—where had the other brash young man got to?—were just of the age of choice, seven years Dahut's junior, newly knighted. Had she asked, either would have followed her to the threshold of the Otherworld and beyond, to say naught of gates of mortal enemies. They would have stormed Bro Érech, would have cut faithless Gwezenneg down upon his very throne. But Father—the wise philosopher king Gralon—had refused to act, and thus the task before her had not been one for blades or spears. Another tack had proved needful to recover her sister and bring retribution down on Gwezenneg of Bro Érech. Dahut was druid trained. She knew the secret names to call upon beings that could aid her when all other routes seemed closed. She knew the words to whisper into the darkest nights, if one truly sought an answer to such calls. A shiver shot through her, a memory of a very dark night, indeed. It was dangerous, calling up the Others. Dangerous, sometimes required.

"I'm ... obliged to make an appearance at the feast first," she said to

Sétanta, her voice raspy. How many goblets had she thrown back? Not enough, if still she could ask the question. "And later to present my sister for the naming ... After that ..." She cupped her hand around the knight's cheek and he shivered. She thought perhaps he was too young to want her, but he leant in and she kissed him, savouring the salty taste of his lips. "Well," she said, pulling away after a long moment. "Well, 'tis a celebration, after all."

"Princess ..."

"Tonight, it's just Dahut. And I do as I wish, with whomever I wish."

His eager nod was almost comical as she rose and slipped away, back toward the main hall, her steps unsteady. Dahut licked her lips in anticipation of the knight's touch. What she had done with Gwezenneg, what she had allowed him to do to her, it left a foul feeling upon her skin, one she longed to lave clean with something pure and her choice.

The great hall danced with the mingling light of a half dozen overhead braziers, all hung from the rafters by iron chains. Marble columns carved with whorling knots supported a high roof, with the rafters threading a maze betwixt the columns. Pigeons, she knew, nested up there, in the hidden recesses, and she smiled recalling a delegate from Starfall Vale who had gotten splattered with droppings whilst in the midst of an address to her father.

The hall was thick with people. None danced, not this night, despite the music and the bard's celebratory song echoing off the vaulted ceiling. Perhaps most of the guests remained uncertain whether to rejoice at the return of the stolen babe or remain in grief over the death of the queen and the prince. Aye, Dahut, too, felt her emotions too moiled to untangle, least of all whilst drunk.

As she returned to the banquet, a tall man intercepted her, well-built, with auburn hair down to his shoulders and piercing eyes, blue as the sea. As deep as the sea, too. "Aodh," she said and bowed. The druid had been one of her instructors and had taught her much of history, math, and the sciences. Sometimes, she thought him the most knowledgeable man she had ever met. Save that he did not share the more obscure arcana. Of the calling of the spirits of the land or of the night, he remained forever reticent, forever obdurate that such a route was too perilous. So she had learnt such craft from others, such as the chief druid Donn himself.

"Princess Dahut." He returned the bow. "Or do we prefer Aveldro, now?"

Dahut struggled to keep her face impassive. Aveldro—the whirlwind. It was the alias she had taken to ensnare Gwezenneg. As his consort, she had found her way to his bed. Which had given her the chance to poison his wine and recover her sister. Of course, to accomplish any of that, she'd needed Otherworldly aid. "Do you fault me for taking steps to protect my family?"

"For protecting your family, never. Those we love define our lives, so naught could matter more. Nor am I one to fault taking on new names as the need arises. No, but Princess, when you bargain with forces from beyond our world, the price may come higher than you imagine. You defied my teachings against such things, though, and now I fear the consequences. There are, always, consequences if one calls up denizens from the Otherworld."

Dahut had little mood for his lectures. "You fear too much. I came away from the bargain with vengeance sated, my sister restored, and myself unscathed." She clapped a hand on his arm in rude dismissal and strode from him, mingling in the party.

Slowly, she worked her way to the back of the hall, where her father sat upon his throne. The chair rested on a dais some half dozen feet above the main floor. A semicircle of candles ran behind the throne, lending an eerie, almost Otherworldly look to its occupant. Her father, for his part, struggled to keep a smile. Dahut wondered how many of the other guests saw his mirth as a veneer. Not that she could begrudge him for mourning her mother and brother; she felt that grief too, like a piece carved out of her gut, leaving her hollow. It left her waking in the middle of the night, gasping, calling for them. But unlike her father, Dahut had resolved to do something about their murders. She could not bring them back from the Otherworld, but she could make certain the one who caused their deaths followed them. The dead cried out for vengeance, and she had not let their cries go unanswered.

As the evening drew on, her father bade her retrieve the babe for the naming ceremony. So, tipsy and thus careful of her steps, she climbed the spiralling stairs to the highest level of the palace. There the royal family of Ys had their chambers, including the babe, though the wet nurse slept in the antechamber of the girl's room. At the moment, the woman lay on a cot by the hearth, snoring. Dahut saw no reason to wake the nurse, who had spent hours tending to a fussy infant, and thus crept past her, into her sister's main room, barely managing to avoid tripping over her own feet in the process.

Then, she stood in the girl's room and blinked, uncertain of what she saw within. There, argent in the moonlight streaming through the window, a red-hooded woman, holding the babe. For a drawn-out moment, Dahut gawped at the very being she had called upon to help her gain her vengeance. "Black Annis ..."

One of the Others, the fae, the creature turned to meet Dahut's gaze. Dahut knew her, had called her up and bargained for the chance to see her sister home, to kill Gwezenneg and escape in the process. And now the Other held Dahut's unnamed baby sister. Did she intend to replace the girl with a changeling? Was that what Dahut had stumbled into?

"R-release her ..." Dahut half commanded, half begged as she stumbled forward, hand raised in denial of this thing, this nightmare.

A malicious gleam filled Black Annis's eyes, like the reflection of firelight that did not exist within the room. "Always a price ..." the Other purred, stepping backward, toward the balcony where a fell wind howled. "An offering of burnt rapunzel flowers?" She snorted, cackled. "Hardly a sufficient price. Your treasure to me you swore." No. Dahut had thought ... had intended to grant her all the gold and silver she could wish for. "All I could carry, said you." Baring her teeth, she hefted the babe with a single hand.

The force of the moment slammed into Dahut like a giant's fist, stole her breath, stole her wits. She flung herself at the Other. But drunken, she tripped, tumbled to the floor. Her head smacked the tiles, dazed her. This could not happen, could not be borne. Not after all she had gone through, all she had given to save her beloved sister. Not ... like ...

Awareness returned like a charging knight, and Dahut pushed herself up, half running, half crawling to the balcony. A stumbling, blurred race, her stomach lurching, threatening to spew out bile Dahut had no time to deal with.

That eerie wind whipped her as she spilled into the empty balcony. Black Annis and the babe were gone as if the night itself had swallowed them. Gone, again.

Knife-sharp grief, dread, shame—they slipped into Dahut's guts, sliced out her insides. All that wine came back up in a torrent, a putrid cataract pouring onto the balcony, silvered by the moonlight. Heedless of the vomit, Dahut dragged herself through the mess, heaved herself up on the balustrade, cast about as if she might spot the vanished Other in the darkness.

But there was naught out there.

Dahut wailed, lost her grip on the rail, and plopped down on her arse, scarce noticing the pain of the impact. The totality of her failure slapped her in the face, mocked her pride. "I will find you," she moaned through her blubbering, drunken sobs. "I will find …"

PART I

Thus, with great Lugus by his side, did Nudd sail against the Tower of Glass, the fomorii hold there to break. His sons beside him—they, armed with bitter iron—Nudd made his war and broke the tower wrought from wondrous pearl. The price came beyond his reckoning, though, for Balor One-Eyed struck down the Lord of the Silver Hand, only to fall himself to wretched Lugus. And as the tower crumbled, so too did the power of the fomorii, forever reduced to dwell only beneath the waves, merrow.
— Lays of Cantref Gwaelod, Canto VII

1

Men have always had a great many names for our kind, or so my grandmother told me. In the Inner Sea, around Pontus, in waters I have never laid eyes upon, they call us sirens. They fear our songs even as they long to hear such music as would touch their souls. In the eastern ocean, so far that tales of those waters are but legends even to us, they name us ninygo or in-eo. In the lands nigh to where I was born, they whisper of the fearsome fomorii of old, who dwell beneath the waves and rise during storms to devour the unwary. But in Cantref Gwaelod, our city beneath the North Sea, we called ourselves merrows.

Though we would have named the shelf upon which our city rests the shallows—for in the shallows merrows find plentiful fish and kelp—our city lies deeper than any human could dive. Even on the clearest day, the water remains dark and turbulent, and no mortal eye will ever chance upon the amber towers of our home, nor linger on the shifting hues of the Coral Palace. Phytoplankton growing within the coral makes the palace gleam such that at night, when merrows become active, my home shines like a beacon calling back any hunters who ventured into distant water for game.

Within the palace, my sisters and I each had our own grottos and our father, King Garanhir, permitted us to decorate them as we saw fit. It pleased him little, I know, that I chose to bedeck my chambers with baubles from the world above. I had gathered jewellery and ornamentation wrought by mortal hands and lost to the sea through violent storms. I had shelves of wooden carvings, which I thought the finest things I had ever laid eyes upon, despite their details having been abraded by the sea. I had arms of bronze cast into the deeps as offerings for the favour of my grandfather, Manawydan, though he was gone from here. I even had found some few iron objects, though like any fae, I found the touch of that metal burned, and regardless, such treasures filled the waters with rust particles. These iron treasures I kept within chests, unwilling to let them go, even as I knew them toxic.

Sometimes, the most precious things are the most harmful to us and we love them all the more for it.

My father blamed his mother, I know, for my perverse—that was a word he used—fascination with the affairs of Men. Since I was young, I recall hearing his fervid lectures decrying the dangers of Man. Men, he claimed, worked iron and would happily turn their foul craft against merrows given the chance. They hated and feared the fae, perhaps not without cause. Our worlds ought not to mix. Men sailed beside Nudd when he came to shatter our Tower of Glass and make us less than once we were. So, Father claimed, we ought have no more love for Men than we did for our landbound fae kindred, the Tylwyth Teg.

This he told his daughters, time and again, though it did not stop my sisters from singing to sailors. Our songs can entrance the mind and leave it pliant as wet sand, and so, like so many merrows before them, the others would draw Men to them. Their hapless victims would vault over the sides of their ships, even in the most turbulent of storm-tossed seas, and drown themselves, all to spend a single instant in the arms of a merrow.

Some of the dead we offered to the Kelpie beneath the great maelstrom of Corryvreckan, for the whirlpool served as the greatest passage between Earth and Faerie, and the Kelpie, the nature spirit who ruled it, was a being ancient and powerful beyond our ken. I do not know what it wished with the dead, or the souls tethered to those bodies, and I think I do not truly wish to know. Some things in the World are best left in the grey places, where we need not dwell on implications that would taste all too bitter.

Most of the dead, however, my sisters would carry home to Cantref Gwaelod. There, in the town square, my fellow merrows would feast upon Man-flesh, would consume the power therein. Flesh holds anáil, the energy of life, even when life has fled it. Sometimes one of my sisters —Mererid, usually, for she was closest to my age—would bid me join in the gorging myself. I never did.

The blood frenzy would come on me, too, as it does all merrows, but I found my gut would churn at the thought of tasting Man-flesh, and I would swim far afield, hunting prey of my own. I could kill an octopus or a seal or even a small shark. I liked prey that would fight back, for the struggle served to soothe the abrasions on my nerves that followed when I denied myself. None of my hunts would quite fill the ache in my belly or the need for the anáil my body craved. So I would wander, alone and at war with my instincts, sometimes for days at a time. My father misliked that even more, especially after he learnt I oft visited the sunken ruins of a fallen human city. But then, that was where I had found the best treasures adorning my grotto, and I would not be swayed from my course.

One night, I was tending to my plot in the palace gardens when the scent of blood came to me, thick and intoxicating. The garden, resplendent with red algae that glow like flame upon the rocks, rings Coral Palace save for a narrow stretch of the approach. My sisters and I each had a plot we would tend. First, we worked under the tutelage of Grandmother Fand; later it became our refuge. The only part of Cantref Gwaelod, outside our grottos, that was ours and ours alone.

Merrows can smell blood from hundreds of feet away and it triggers something primal in us: the blood frenzy. Sharklike teeth descend in our mouths as the instinct to attack and devour takes hold. Can a merrow fight the blood frenzy? Yes. There is savagery in our natures, for certain, but we are more than mere sharks. Still, it means a war against oneself, and such wars take their toll.

So, already, ere ever I heard Mererid, I knew what they had brought. "Lí Ban!" she shouted, pitching the Voice so the water would carry it from the town square to the palace. "Lí Ban, a squall capsized a ship out of Inis Fáil, and the deep claimed a dozen lives. Hurry, before the choice bits are gone!"

Sometimes, I think my sisters never noticed that I fled from such feasts they arranged, whilst other times I assumed they feigned ignorance to avoid confrontation. Either way, I scurried from Cantref Gwaelod, hating myself for my roiling emotions. I could neither stand the thought of eating Men nor push the sickening desire to do so from my mind, and thus every moment spent in the presence of the feast became a torment.

It was long while before I was far enough away from Cantref Gwaelod to no longer catch the scent of blood, and longer still before I could force my fangs to recede. Though the sea teems with life, there is a quiet beneath the waves unless you draw close to merrow encampments or dolphin pods or other intelligent creatures. Across vast expanses, alone, the experience becomes almost akin to being deprived of a sense. In the city, the water carries an endless procession of sounds and scents to us, and we quickly develop an instinct to block unwanted stimuli from our minds until we no longer notice them. Leastwise, not until they're gone. Once far enough away from the bustle, though, a sense of solitude tends to creep upon one. It seizes you with the force of a riptide, and you realise that you were both a part of a greater organism and something separate, complete unto yourself. Or so I found myself thinking as I swam the hours-long journey toward my sunken treasure trove.

I passed a pod of humpback whales, larger than most pods, almost a score of the majestic behemoths. I know they sensed me, for such creatures miss little, but I held back and they did not shy from me. Their song filled the sea, mournful as any threnody of my people, bemoaning the loss of our golden days. We always felt loss. Always the impression, handed down from the elders, that once we had been more than we were now. In those days, it was said, we had ruled the sea and land and passed through either, whilst Men thought us gods. Sometimes, tales blamed the elders who had led us astray. Sometimes, they cast imprecations upon the youth, as though our weak hearts led to the enervation of our race. Mostly, though, they blamed Nudd, and the dwellers of the surface, for having denied us the ability to assume legged form, when the Tower of Glass was broken.

If our people thought we had once been more, I imagine Men felt much the same about themselves. I came to the ruin. The sunken city was silent monument to the fragile glories of Man. Vast edifices of granite surrounded the complex, crumbling and breached in many locations. It had taken me a great deal of musing to realise the wall must have served defensive purposes on land, where humans could not have just swum over it, as I did now. Perhaps they had built the barrier to ward against the fae—or at least our distant kin, the Tylwyth Teg—or perhaps to protect themselves from other Men. That, I suppose, I would never know.

"Men," Grandmother had once said, "tend to think of the Earth as immutable. But the land and sea remain forever in flux when measured against the span of Ages. Shores that once stood high above the water erode, oceans rise or fall, and even the continents are reshaped across eons. Thus, in hubris or self-delusion, do Men raise their cities and imagine they will endure in perpetuity. But life is change, Lí Ban, and naught lasts forever."

Those of us who dwelt beneath the sea, we knew change was constant, the World itself ebbing and flowing like tides. Endurance was adaptation. I wondered, then, what would lead Men to think they could build something that would remain unchanging, in defiance of the very order of nature.

I found myself swimming over ruined halls and imagining that here, mortal princes and fair maidens had once dined or danced, and there, great and weighty councils were held by kings. I would dart through the countless buildings of the ruined city and muse over if one might have housed the horses Men were said to have tamed, or if another building might have been home to the infamous forges of a great smith. For, of all the arts of Man, none were stranger or more forbidden to us than that of metallurgy. The Tylwyth Teg—our land-based fae cousins—had their own smiths, of course, but they worked in bronze or fabled adamant. For us, though, we touched metal only when such things fell into the sea. Our spears were carved of bone or coral, our tools of sharpened obsidian.

Whenever I came to these ruins, curiosity about mortal lands and customs and creativity sent my heart fluttering. Time fell away, and I could spend hours darting through these shadowed, crumbling halls in what felt the space of moments. Now, I came to a room where the floor had cracked, revealing an opening to another space below. Perched on the edge of it, my tail brushing over worn flagstones, I peered into the darkness. Merrow eyes see well in the dark—we are nocturnal by nature—but even I could make out little in the black that welled like ink below me.

I knew, of course, it was foolhardy to imagine venturing into a crevice where eels or other dangers might lurk unseen. In my mind, I could see them writhing down there, daring me to wriggle through the gap. I knew I ought to flee from here. In truth, I should have returned home, for by now, my sisters would have begun to worry, my father would have grown cross, and even Grandmother might be losing some of her indulgence. But what wonders of a fallen civilisation might lie in wait just beyond that threshold?

Eel-like myself, I squeezed into the opening. My tail snagged upon the jagged stones, edges peeling off some scales. The pain had me gritting my teeth, but I had no easy way to back up, so I forced myself downward. The edge scraped my fluke and though I could not see the swirls of blood in the water, I could smell them. The piercing awareness of one's own spilled blood, rather than triggering a frenzy, instead tends to leave a merrow enraged, ready to fight anyone at hand. In this case, I had no one to lash out at.

I drifted down to the floor and bunched up my tail so I could probe at it with gentle fingers. The flesh was raw and painful but not mangled, Elder Deep be praised. With a ruined fluke, a merrow becomes the subject of derision, unable to swim at speed or hunt for themselves. Sometimes these things healed, but it could mean months of shame. Oh, as the king's daughter, I knew few outside my family would mock me to my face. No, but I would feel their whispers as I swam past, and I would know they snickered over the marring of my beauty. No one ever claimed the sea, or its children, were compassionate.

We saw our tails as emblems of our allure—only our hair counted higher, in fact—and few things matter more to merrows than being alluring. My tail was an iridescent silver flecked with gold, and though I oft earned compliments, I found myself sometimes resentful of the thing. Without this tail, I could have climbed on land and studied Man for myself. I could have passed for one of them, as was said of some of our cousins in other waters. Grandmother claimed tails were blessings from the Elder Deep, the slumbering goddess of Naunet in the Otherworld, and thus we ought to praise her for the gift. With tails, we could swim faster and farther than our legged cousins. I could have, had I the mettle and need, visited the Eternal Depths of the Otherworld and sought the lost histories of my kindred.

But it was not the deepest, farthest seas I longed to look upon but forests and mountains and the cities of Man. And the chance to venture there was lost with the breaking of the Tower of Glass. It shattered, and so too did the merrows of the North Sea. We had been diminished, denied the land we once had ruled, fomorii no longer.

Content that my tail had suffered no lasting harm, I patted around the room, searching for plunder to make the injury worthwhile. My fingers brushed over shards of something smooth with ragged edges. A jar, perhaps? Whatever it was, it was broken. If I found naught better, I'd take a piece with me to study later, but I'd have little joy of ruined goods. Close to the floor, dragging myself by my hands, I crawled about the room until my hand landed on something of carved stone. It was almost as smooth as the shards but with more detail. By touch, I examined the groves and rises, trying to picture what I'd happened across. Was it ... a face? A statue?

I hefted the object under one arm, needing only a trickle of my anáil to enhance my strength. Content with my prize, I squeezed out from the opening—with greater care this time—and made my egress from the human palace. Once outside, bands of silver moonlight filtering through the water allowed me to examine what I'd found. It was indeed a carving of a woman, wrought in marble, standing roughly as tall as my two hands. Flecks of pigment told me the makers had once painted it, though years beneath the sea had worn away the paint and no doubt some of the details as well. Nevertheless, the object was beautiful and I found myself tracing my fingers along the recessions of the eyes. The artist had even carved receded lids over those, and little flecks of green paint remained in the irises as well.

Who had this person been, I wondered? Someone important, for

Men to go to such lengths to immortalise her features in stone. Someone venerated for her beauty? For her bloodline? For her deeds?

The carving seemed primed to speak to me, eager almost, to whisper to me of a life led, of passions burning bright before they were snuffed out. Unable to help myself, I held the statue to my ear, imagining it would speak. But, of course, if the past speaks to us through the objects it left behind, it does not do so with words. And I was late enough that I would find trouble on my return as it was. So, statue once more under my arm, I began the long swim home.

"YOUR FATHER WAS ready to have you tied down over this," Grandmother said the moment I swam into my grotto. How long had the woman lingered in my space, awaiting my return?

With a grunt, I deposited my new statue in a corner for further study later. I had no way to confirm any conclusions I might draw from these objects—oh, and I pondered their purpose, their origins, and whether they had proved dear or prosaic to the land-dwellers—but that would not stop me from trying to learn all I could. I wondered who those people had been, what their lives had been like, and why they had abandoned so many of their creations when the sea swallowed their home. I stared into the deep green of those eyes and imagined I knew the woman. I fancied she would, if I waited long enough, speak to me of her life.

Content with the statue's position, I turned to face my grandmother, arms folded over my chest. I did not speak, however, mainly because we both knew any such threat my father had made was an idle one. No merrow would imprison another. The ocean may not have been kind, may sometimes have been cruel; but to stop another from swimming where they willed would have been an act far worse than murder.

Grandmother soon gave over the pretence of threat, blowing bubbles in a huff. "Well. Leastwise, he asked me to speak to you on this matter. You went again to those ruins." She waved a hand toward my recovered artefact, making plain any denial was pointless. The woman worked her jaw a moment, her gaze taking in the wound on my tail. From the set of her mouth, her shark-teeth had at least partially descended, a testament to how much I had vexed my family this time. That, more than any castigation, had me worried.

"Grandmother—"

"That city was destroyed because of the faithlessness of Man, and yet you persist in your obsession with their treacherous ways, Lí Ban. A scholarly interest is one thing, but I grow concerned that you drift toward full-blown obsession with Man. The younger race, though weak, is treacherous."

Perhaps I ought to have lingered on her warning, but something else in her words piqued my interest. "That city ... You know what happened to those ruins! I thought the land collapsed into the sea over time, but you imply it happened more swiftly than that."

Grandmother's opalescent eyes nictitated in a show of her frustration. "It is a fell place, best avoided, child. Besides its own dangers, it lies dangerously close to coasts where human vessels sail. You've no business there. It would be better for you to cast aside this fancy." A pause. "Your father thinks it perhaps time to find you a mate. He said that mayhap a babe in your belly would temper your wild impulses."

I sputtered at that, indignant. "I've not yet passed seventeen winters, Grandmother!" By merrow standards, I was not even an adult, though Grandmother had told me stories of human girls mated younger than that—not that she'd ever reveal how she knew such things, though I half suspected she had lived in the time of the Tower of Glass. Grandmother said mortal couples made oaths of lifelong matings because they liked to torture themselves should their natural instincts guide them away from their chosen mate. I found a macabre fascination in imagining girls—children, in fact—forced to make decisions that would bind them for their entire lives. This idea of marriage struck me as much akin to holding someone prisoner and stealing their will. Only fools made oaths. Only sorcerers, their souls abraded by the evil of their Art, deigned to *strip* the will from another intelligent being. Even death was better than the denial of choice.

I shook my head. "I've no wish for a mate. Surely Father would not force me to take one?"

The old merrow held my gaze, her tail churning the water of my grotto. I could not be certain what roil of thought and emotion unfolded behind the pearls of her eyes. I had vexed her, I knew, but was there more? I had the sensation a part of her found my recalcitrance refreshing, as if I dared swim down channels she wished she had the courage to chance, long back. Was it the regret of age I sensed, or was this rather the arrogance of youth in thinking I could know the mind of one who had lived for centuries more than I had? Whatever the case, my grandmother did not enlighten me.

"He may not force you to choose a mate, Lí Ban," she said after the moment had drawn out long enough to become painful. "But if you defy his will oft enough, you may find this palace becomes less welcoming than that to which you have become accustomed. A princess who pays no heed to the wishes of her kin may find they respond in kind."

I balked, the weight of her words slamming into me with the force of a dolphin's charge. "He would exile me?" Such things were rare, mentioned more in whispers than put into practice. A single merrow, alone in the merciless depths of the sea ... Even if predators, demons of the deep, or—as was like to happen—other merrow clans did not slay them, they would face the slow decay of their minds. For alone, unable to give voice to one's thoughts, denied companionship, madness must surely impend. For how long could one sing to oneself alone?

Mererid once told me a tale, from long before our time, of a mermaid driven out due to greed, after she sought, time and again, to claim treasures from others. Whilst no one knew what became of her, in the tale Mererid told, the mermaid went to the Kelpie in search of a new life. The capricious sea spirit gave it to her, aye, by casting her into the Otherworld.

Sorrow creased Grandmother's features, no longer hard to read but rather drooping her whole visage. "Let us not find out. His cares for you, spurned long enough, could become anger; I have seen it happen between parents and children more oft than I wish. Bend a little before you wind up breaking your father."

When she left my grotto, I found myself leaning against the wall. I stole glances at the artefacts I had gathered from the ruins, thinking on how much I treasured them and the stories they held. Yet neither did I wish to vex my father, and I could not stop playing Grandmother's words over in my mind, time and again.

Frustrated, I curled my tail around the marble statue and leant on my arms, staring at the fine carving. Finally, I allowed myself to sleep.

I WAS ON LAND, *had legs. Was dancing in a candlelit hall. Not strange, as it ought to have been, but wonderful, a dream longed for, now fulfilled. There was music, lively, haunting. Melodies soaring, echoing off vaulted ceilings. I could have sung better, but that thought was distant.*

Now, I was swaying, whirling about, felt the rush of wind over my cheeks as I turned. Felt the warmth of a hall filled with hundreds of burning candles sending wisps of smoke skyward, a hall filled with close-pressed bodies. Their heady scents filled the air, thick as the music, intoxicating, alluring.

Men, women in their fine, brightly coloured garb. Smiles and laughter and eagerness and lust. So many scents I knew, longed to know. The women had ankle-length garments that caught the air as they turned, seemed to take flight on breezes they themselves created. The men wore separate pieces on torsos and legs. Both sexes had coverings on their feet, the women's nigh hidden by their clothes. Almost everyone wore golden rings upon their arms, bands glittering in the firelight, speaking of lavish evenings I both knew and did not.

Everything had grown so foreign, so strangely familiar. Here I was, living among them, dancing the night away as I had yearned to do for so long. I knew the steps. Legs I had never possessed followed impenetrable rhythms as natural as the beat of my tail carrying me through the waters. I wanted to leap, to run, to squeal with delight, but my body refused to break from the dance. It was me, but not.

A man came, finer garbed than the rest, a golden torc around his neck. It was twisted, like the ropes on human ships, intricately worked with a craftsmanship no merrow could replicate. He took my hand, danced with me, spun me. Kissed me on the cheek. His long moustache tickled.

I laughed, my heart soaring. I wasn't bound by legs at all. "Leaving Mother without her partner?"

The man glanced back at another woman. Grace and pride, all wrapt in a flowing gown of crimson, vibrant as the sea anemones of my garden. I could scarce imagine her walking in that. She more floated across the hall, weaving between dancers, agile as a minnow. Lines creased her face, around the eyes, around the mouth, but somehow, I thought it a good thing. Knew them as marks of a life well lived, prizes more valuable than any artefact bedecking my grotto.

A young man drifted by her side, whispered something in her ear. Gently, she shoved him toward a trio of giggling girls who hid their mouths behind their hands. I didn't know why they hid their mirth. Didn't know, yet in the dream, I knew. This veneer was part of the game, the boy wanting to peel it away, layer by layer. The girls wanting him to succeed.

The man I danced with broke away with a bow, making room for a younger man. The new one swept a deeper bow, took my fingers and kissed them. "May I?"

Oh, indeed. Indeed. My heart beat faster, so fast I could feel the pulse in my neck. His eyes glinted with life, with passion.

It was a dream ... all I had ever dreamt of coming alive.

Somewhere, in the distance, scarce audible over the music, a babe was squalling.

I AWAKENED on the floor of my grotto, both hands wrapt around the statue as though I thought to throttle it. A long time I lay there, staring into the unknown depths of its green eyes, wondering how it could have sparked so strange a dream, at once both vivid and surreal. Had I so yearned to walk among Men that my slumbering mind now conjured phantasms of life there? For there were elements of my dream which I could not trace back to my studies, details I could only imagine pure fancy. For what knew I of fancy gowns and mortal music, of smoky halls filled with burning wood scents, or the smell of Men? How could I have known faces of people I had not before seen?

And yet, and yet, and yet ...

Incipient thoughts tugged at me like clinging seaweed, rendering my motions sluggish, my moods distracted as I went through my night. I tended my garden, positioning a sea anemone just so, to further enhance the impression of growing flames around the palace. Yet, whilst most evenings I would have revelled in the chance to imagine fire, instead I caught myself imagining, time and again, returning to my grotto. I longed to slip back into the dream, to glean more from its parade of strange images. Surreal though it had been, it seemed to hold more substance than the waking trance in which I now found myself.

Even before sunrise, I slunk off to my chambers, curled around the statue, and fell into stroking its carven hair as I let my mind drift. Eyes, green as burgeoning algae ...

❧

THE MAN I had seen in my dream—my father there, though not my father—stood with me upon a rooftop, as did the woman, my mother, and not. Beyond a balustrade, the palace fell away, revealing a many-tiered city of white stone, rising from a lowland plain. In the dream, I knew the sight as I knew my own hands, yet I could not place it, familiar though it seemed.

The man held in his hands a painted marble statue, set it on a pedestal amongst two others of its kind. Each was perhaps the length of my forearm, carved with intricate detail and highlighted by vibrant colours. The one the man placed now was a woman, clad in a dress as blue as the sea. Was that why it called me?

Was that why it ...?

But it was me, somehow I knew, looking into those striking green eyes. It was me, little though I could explain or fathom such. I leant closer, examining it, knowing the other two were my parents, I thought. Aye, including the man who had just set this piece.

"All as it should be," the man said, and I looked to my parents.

There was another pedestal. It would have another statue there, I knew, with uncanny insight. Who ... the boy I had seen in the dance. My ... brother ...

My mother smiled, laugh lines once more creasing her mouth, her eyes. A moment so perfect.

Too perfect.

Something was wrong.

The sky turned the loathsome colour of iron. Thunder rumbled, fulgurations crackling through dark clouds.

I looked back.

My mother's body lay upon the ground, blood spattered, limbs skewed at odd angles. Head hewn from her shoulders. Beside her, my brother lay in similar state, he too decapitated.

A shift.

I rode like the wind, skirting the coast, racing down the trail. Not just the wind, the whirlwind, sweeping down with promise. My hair streamed behind me, my cloak tugging at my neck as it flew.

My heart raced, eagerness so sharp I could taste it. There is joy in speed, in the pounding of pulses, in the rush of life.

There is wrath when it is stolen. There is grief.

No grief could show upon my face, as I drew nigh to the city along the shore. Open gates and open arms awaited me, an embrace. I did not want to dwell on that either.

There would be feasting and music, laughter, and dancing. The press of bodies, the rush of wine. The closeness that would follow in private rooms. Not so many months back, I had danced with Father in our own hall, and laughed and smiled, a lifetime ago.

Another shift, my vision changed. Only a hint of a trail before me, barely visible in the torchlight, but I knew the way. A moonless night. A time of peril, when good folk would hide behind iron-barred doors. I was not them, if ever I had been.

I walked through the darkened wood, my hood thrown back, a basket of flowers on my arm. In the distance, wolves were howling. Scents of loam and petrichor made the forest seem fresh, as if mocking the darkness of my heart.

A faint rumble of thunder crackled somewhere far away; that iron sky. I cast a glance overhead—wondered if the Wild Hunt rode—though I could see naught through the canopy. I would not fear. Not this night.

Bodies without heads. Souls in agony, caught betwixt this world and the other.

Onward, along the rough path. I should not be here, had to be.

Before me, the nemeton—sacred grove—opened, centred around the great oak, fallen now. Lightning blasted, its stump a husk. A memory. An altar, long used in days—nights—when a certain operation became needful.

I paced around the periphery of the clearing. The oak, it had been massive, thicker around than my arm span. Its roots ran, ran wide, grasping and choking through the soil. It had prevented other trees from growing too nigh this place, had created something sacred.

THIS WENT ON FOR DAYS, and I dared to fancy that, in holding the statue, I had indeed touched the mind of this other woman. That I had entered her life and saw myself as her. Had these things really happened, I wondered, even as I struggled to ascribe meaning or order to what my dreams revealed. I would wake late, after sunset. Spurning the choice to hunt with my sisters or Father's knights, I would break my fast only on what kelp or shellfish were at hand. Then I would pass the night in a daze, perhaps interrogating Grandmother for details about the surface world, or perhaps venturing there. Once, I returned to the sunken ruins and claimed discs of gold and of bronze whose purpose I could not ascertain. These, too, I filed into my grotto, displaying them on my shelves like prizes won.

Mostly, though, I awaited sunrise and the chance to drift once more into the vivid imaginings that had touched my soul. I ate less and less, though I knew my sisters had begun to notice, perhaps even to be concerned.

"Are you in love?" Mererid asked, having cornered me in an alcove of the Coral Palace from which I could not escape short of shoving her. "Is it to some diurnal trysts you have begun sneaking off to? Because I do not think Father will begrudge you anyone you wish to dally with. Unless ... not a lowborn, is it?" She must have read the look of shock on my face, for she quickly shook her head. "No, of course not. A knight, perhaps? Oh ... It's Morag, I warrant! Aye, I saw his gaze lingered upon your tail in the hunt last month."

"It is not!" I protested, with perhaps a hair too much vehemence. "I mean, I have no lover, Mererid, least of all Morag."

She shrugged, though the twinkle in her eyes made it plain she remained unconvinced. While older merrows have eyes which turn opalescent, in our youth, our eyes are human-like, save for the vibrance of our irises. Mererid had luminous eyes, pale as summer kelp and full of mischief. She had told me my own eyes were amber, as if I myself were a piece of the great towers of Cantref Gwaelod. But then, perhaps that was the sort of thing a sister says when she strives to make someone feel connected to something.

"Perhaps you should try one, then? Ailbert, mayhap?"

"Did Father put you up to this?" I demanded, suddenly remembering what Grandmother had said. How many days had that been? A fortnight, perhaps. Waking and sleeping seemed to bleed together now, and time had lost its shape as I wandered, again and again in lands of dream. I grabbed Mererid's upper arms to guide her aside so I could swim around her. "I told you, I've no need for a lover! And I'll thank you to keep your fins out of my affairs!"

I ought not to have shouted at her, a point her glower drove home. No doubt others in the palace would have heard my outburst. Embarrassed, I darted around the corner and sped out the first window I came to. I could not stand to face Mererid, much less see the sneers of our servants at how I'd spoken to her. Deep! She probably even meant well by me, but I could not stand the thought of any of them trying to influence my decisions, much less pair me with a mate of their choosing.

Knowing I was being petulant, I swam from Cantref Gwaelod. At first, I headed for the ruins, as they had become my refuge. I felt fair certain that the woman whose life I viewed had hailed from there, in a time ere the waves swallowed the place. The sunken city was massive. Had someone come looking for me, they mostlike would not have found me. Besides, no one else ventured so far from our own city, least of all alone. There were sharks and giant squid and behemoths in the deep, to say naught of the danger of drawing too close to the Corryvreckan where dwelt the Kelpie. Others would have named my sojourns pointless risks.

Instead of following the seabed to reach the ruins, however, I eventually found myself swimming upward. Perhaps I saw the shadow of the human vessel passing far above before my mind realised what I'd chanced upon. Curiosity clamped upon me like the jaws of a great white, and there was no more freeing myself from its grip than there would have been from so fearsome a predator. Mortal vessels sailed these waters sometimes, aye, but I had seen few and, ere now, always heeded Father's command to avoid them. Before caution could have me thinking better of it, I breached the surface alongside the ship, close enough to spy on the mortals.

Over the crashing waves, I heard the sounds of raucous laughter and wailing. It took me a moment to realise men were singing off-key, and I could only grimace at the mockery they made of music. Every merrow has the Voice, and I could have sung to them such songs as would have made them weep. I wanted to, to share my gift and show them the fathomless beauty of *true* song. But I knew that was how many a sailor had drowned, for my own sisters had made it so. Men could lose their minds over the songs of the sea and cast themselves in the wakes of their ships without thought for their safety.

If it was a terrible thing to deny another merrow their will, how could it not be woeful to do so to a mortal? I knew others thought the younger race so much lesser than the Elder Races, accounting them of no more import than beasts. Giants and fae, we were stronger and much longer lived than these mortals. We were connected to powers they lacked, possessed of knowledge that, according to Grandmother, Men could not dream of fathoming. But did that mean their wills and lives meant no more than those of carp?

I did not want to be responsible for their deaths and, unlike my sisters, I had no desire to feast on their flesh—or leastwise none I would ever act upon. So, rather than sing for them, I listened. I soaked in their mirth as waves lapped over me, letting vicarious joy balm my soul from aches I had never understood. For an hour or more I swam alongside their ship as it threaded the waters, looking both majestic and so fragile, heaved about by forces below that the Men could neither see nor understand. It was this vast bulk, whale-like, and yet unliving, a foreign intruder in these waters. A time or thrice I dared touch it, savouring the feel of wet planks beneath my fingers, even of the barnacles crusted upon the underside of the hull. How could this thing, this dead—by all appearances decaying—enormity serve as a bastion of life to these Menfolk? I felt I had strayed into dream, unable to believe I had allowed myself to draw so very close to these beings, forbidden as they were.

As time passed, I picked up a few of their names, and though I stifled my laughter lest they detect me, I found myself snickering at their jests, some innocent and some lewd. If any of the sailors should chance to peer over the rail of their vessel, I would duck beneath the waters and pop up in another location. Once, I saw a man point in my direction. When I resurfaced, I heard others ribbing him for his vivid imagination. "Donall's seeing mermaids now!" one of them cried, evoking chortles from a dozen others. Their language sounded odd to my ears, not least because their voices were ferried through air rather than water. Still, like most fae, I had the gift of Tongues and could understand all spoken languages.

"Too long without a woman, then?" another jibed.

"Uh ... aye," Donall admitted, and I allowed myself a knowing smirk. If only they guessed I was about, that the merrows did indeed lurk in the shallows off their shores, I imagine they would have treated the young man with more respect for his perceptiveness.

Oh, but Father thought it behoved us to allow Men to all but forget our existence. They would find merrows hard prey to hunt, true, but we gained little from allowing them to try. Besides, as he explained to my chagrin, so long as Men doubted our existence, it made it easier for *us* to prey on *them*. We were fables—fancies conjured by the minds of lonely sailors—and as such, they did not seek to ward against our existence. They thought the fomorii legends of a cloudy past, perhaps never connected our kind to the feared tyrants of their ancient stories. They did not call their druids for protections, nor hurl iron javelins at every possible sighting of our kind. Father aimed to keep it that way.

Such laws meant that we did not reveal ourselves to any Man, save those we intended to drown. And I hid, skulking in the dark, whilst wishing I could show my face to these people. In a single eve they might answer a thousand questions about life on the surface. They might expand my knowledge a hundredfold with thoughtful conversation. More, they could have lent meaning to the strange dreams that now plagued my sleep. Was this woman I saw real, as I believed her to be? Had she lived in the now fallen city? Could I, in inquiring about her, about that place, understand what was happening to me? But such contact was forbidden, and by trailing them without drawing them to their dooms, already I skirted the edge of Father's laws.

"Too many of our kind fell in the days of Nudd," Grandmother had told me once when explaining why Father remained so insistent that we not reveal ourselves to Men. "'Twas Men who shattered the Tower of Glass and, with it, our greatest glories." I wondered, at the time, if such events had to do with the disappearance of her mate, Manawydan, though asking would have seemed too crass. None, in my hearing, had ever mentioned Fand's lost mate in front her. "They are transitory creatures," Grandmother said. "Short of life and short of memory. Let them forget."

The human vessel drew nigh upon a pebbled strand, and I had no choice save to fall back or risk discovery. Besides, their ship had sailed perilously close to the Corryvreckan. Perhaps in their celebration, they had not realised how nigh they chanced to the maelstrom, or perhaps they, so long as they remained free of the current, thought they would keep safe. Only later did I learn they thought it a game—they might prove their mettle by chancing as close to the pull of that vortex as they could and still break free. Men, as I learnt then, could be fools.

I was far from them, yet still I heard their cry upon seeing a horse wandering by on that strand. I knew of such animals from my studies—or mostly from inquiring with the elders like Grandmother, really—and they held a certain fascination, so I swam closer than perhaps I ought to have done. The creature had a dappled grey and black coat, so dark it seemed almost to shimmer beneath the moonlight. Something—perhaps a glint in its eye—raised my hackles and a sickening foreboding clenched my gut.

Already, many of the men had taken a small boat ashore and were approaching the animal. I watched, floating near the surface, dread rising over me. I wanted to cry out to them, to warn them of the apprehension that had seized me, but doing so would have violated the laws of Cantref Gwaelod. How was I to defy my father for the sake of Men? Instead, I clenched my hands into fists and silently whispered across the waves, begging them to turn back, knowing the beast they approached as Otherworldly. Should I try to turn the Voice on them? Compel them to save themselves?

But no, they began to mount the creature, though its back ought not to have held six men. I shook my head and reached a helpless hand out to the humans, knowing what would happen. For I had heard the legends in my childhood, though I had not given much thought to the many forms the Kelpie might choose to take. It was, so far as I understood, a manifestation of the Corryvreckan; a spirit of nature more ancient and powerful than any merrow, even the great elders like my grandfather, Manawydan. No merrow dared approach the waters of the Kelpie save in supplication, bearing offerings of drowned mortals. But perhaps it did not subsist only on the tribute we offered. Why could it not claim its own due, should mortals be fool enough to draw nigh?

Like a receding riptide, the Kelpie burst into motion, racing across the sea. Its hooves flung a curtain of water behind it as it ran, and the men on it screamed, belated terror grasping them at last. Too late, by far. The Kelpie had them in its power now, and their hands stuck to it as it rushed at their waiting ship.

Contact was forbidden; I ought to have swum home with all the speed I could have mustered and then some, but instead, I lurked, watching the macabre ending of those humans who had so ensnared my thoughts. The wake the Kelpie generated slammed into the side of the ship, becoming a rogue wave that flung the vessel far out to sea. Outward … and directly into the tides of the Corryvreckan. The ship listed to one side and I watched as the mast snapped in twain, broken like a toy. Sails and rigging caught in the whirlpool, further yanking the ship downward until the vessel capsized. Every last Man on that ship was about to have their soul sucked down to the Otherworld. They were dead, even as those on the back of the Kelpie would soon be dead. Almost as if in response to my thoughts, the horse banked, reared, and dove beneath the waves.

Something broke in me. Whatever force had held me there shattered, and before I could think better of it, I darted toward where the Kelpie now swam for the Corryvreckan itself. The spirit no doubt could have made better time, but I got the sense it was drawing out the drowning, feasting upon the Men's fear as much as it would upon their bodies and souls. Its cruelty gave me the chance I needed to catch up and I seized one of the men, yanking him from the beast.

Or I tried. His left hand remained tangled in the Kelpie's seaweed-like mane, stuck fast. Not even my merrow strength, enhanced by anáil, allowed me to tug his arm free. The Man looked at me, and I recognised Donall. Stark terror blanched his features. He choked upon his scream, sucking in a lungful of water. The churning maelstrom nigh blinded me, its currents threatening to send me careening into the vortex. In the space of a few more pounding heartbeats, these people would be sucked into the Otherworld, and I dared go no further or risk being pulled in myself. The transition would not kill me, my essence being of Faerie, but I had little wish to explain myself to the Kelpie who very well might feast on my soul for the trespass.

I knew I ought to have let him go. Having swallowed that much water, he was already drowned. I should have fled. Instead, I summoned my shark teeth and bit off the fingers of his left hand. His blood triggered the frenzy in me. I wrapt my arms around him and, with several beats of my tail, sent the both of us shooting away from the maelstrom. Every instinct screamed at me to feast upon the bleeding hunk of prey cradled against my breast. My fangs were a hair from his face, and I wanted to bite it so badly it was a physical ache, the need of it tearing me apart.

I cannot say whence I drew the strength to resist, but rather than bite him, I directed all my frenetic energy into my tail and hurled us above the water, bursting into the sky like a breaching whale. The Man no longer breathed. That much I realised in the space of time we remained airborne before crashing back into the water. Still, I did not release him nor set to feasting, much though my body craved it. Instead, I carried him to shore, on the very pebbled strand where he and his fellows had wrought their doom.

On the beach I sang, using the Voice to issue a command to any vestige of his soul yet within his body. It was a simple mandate, but an urgent one: *breathe.*

He did. Though the first breath was more a matter of retching up a torrent of seawater, and the next few were interrupted by bouts of violent coughing. Would he now live? Was that sufficient to have saved him from the Kelpie? If he did survive, would he recall he had laid eyes upon a merrow? That she had saved him?

My heart swore I had done a good thing. Yet I had violated the law of my people and I could not imagine how Father would react should he learn of this. Exile? It seemed probable, as I had now gone leagues farther than any of my previous acts of defiance. Perhaps I would even deserve it, had I brought woe upon my fellow merrows by revealing our existence to Men once more.

Yet, I refused to let this man perish. He tossed about as if feverish, so I stroked his brow and whispered soothing nonsense, though I had little idea how to tend to a human. Blood still oozed from the stubs of his fingers and, for a moment, I dwelt upon the inherent savagery that lurked in my breast. Would a human have imagined saving the man by biting off his fingers? Could a Man even have done so? Deep! I whimpered, not knowing what to do, and cast about for any ideas.

Far down the strand, on the fringes of a grove of trees, I saw a human structure. If there were others of his own kind there, they might know how to attend to his injuries. I doubted taking him back into the water would do him much good, but neither could I get him to the building without swimming closer. So I slung the man around my back and wriggled into the sea, careful to keep his lolling head above the waves and praying to the Elder Deep that would be enough to stop him from swallowing more of the ocean.

It was slow going, swimming like that, and time and again I found myself straining to look over my shoulder, wondering if I had killed poor Donall after all. At last I reached the beach beneath that structure, and my heart fell. For it seemed more a circle of standing stones than any home or estate in which Men might dwell. Perhaps it served a religious purpose? I could not otherwise guess at the intent of raising those menhirs like that, amid the trees. I had never come so close to the shore afore now and under other circumstances, I would have revelled in the chance to ogle the vibrant green leaves that sprouted from the upper reaches of those plants.

But Donall was shivering—lacking merrow tolerance for the cold of the sea—fitful, and I could feel his soul threatening to untether from its mortal shell. It is a strange sensation, one I think only those whose essences are bound to the Otherworld can experience, being in the presence of one close to death. Dawn had broken over the horizon, a violent flame pushing back the purple bruise of the sky. If no Men lurked nigh, Donall would die before the sun had finished casting away the night.

"Help!" I shrieked, not knowing what else to do. "Help him! Help him!" I knew my cries would prove in vain, but I had to do something. I had to *try*.

Though I had all but given over hope, a female face peeked out from the grove. She was clad in white garments and began looking about for the source of the cries. I could not allow her to see me—saving Donall, whose claims of merrow might be dismissed as delirium, was already a crime—so I hunched down and slipped back into the sea. After I had swum a safe distance, I watched while a trio of Men came rushing to find the man I had rescued from the Kelpie.

Two of them lifted Donall and began to scale back toward the structure. The woman lingered, casting looks about, across the sea. Searching for me? I did not know, but if I dawdled, she might spot me. So I darted beneath the waves and sped from there.

I TRIED to push the Man from my mind, and with him, the guilt I felt over having broken Father's law. I had allowed a mortal to glimpse me and live! Much though I told myself he could not have known what he saw in the chaos and the terror of his drowning, I could never be certain of it. I thought it better to ignore the whole event, go on with my gardening and my hunting and the banalities of life in Cantref Gwaelod.

But the dreams came again, more vividly. Visions of a life on land, of dancing and dining and laughter all paraded through my mind in gossamer panoplies, the shifting from one instant to the next so sharp as to defy any sort of understanding, and yet compelling. I *wanted* to fall into those moments; I wanted it to the pith of my soul. That life that could never have been, it seemed so close I could have touched it. At least until I opened my eyes.

I WAS MOUNTED, riding a mare. Wind tugged on my hair, had it streaming behind me as I skirted a city. 'Twas a place I knew well in the dream and thought perhaps I knew as myself as well.

The long seawall glistened in the morning sun, the granite slick with brine and last night's rains. Now, at low tide, the walls rose some two hundred feet above sea level, a vast arm beckoning me home. There were slingers on the walls, watching me approach, unconcerned. No Man could dare assault this place. I knew it had other defences, too, couldn't recall what. The isthmus, the tide … it warded this place, somehow.

Clutching a babe to my breast, I cantered the length of the wall, toward the fortified gate. There were men there; they seemed to recognise me. "Princess," each said, their heads bowed as I passed, though I barely slowed at the gate, so intent was I to get the child home. My sister, I knew, though how I could not say. I knew it, knew her down to the depth of my soul.

Past the gatehouse, a green plain ran the length of the isthmus. Farmers cultivated the rich soil, raising vineyards or patches of cauliflower or plots for onions and garlic. Golden fields of barley lined the cobbled path leading to the city. Field hands bowed and waved as I passed, but I paid them even less mind than I had the guards. My sister was so young, the girl did not even have a name, as yet. Nameless, she was vulnerable, could be taken and replaced with a changeling, but names had to be given with due ceremony. The girl needed the care of a wet nurse, and she needed one now, for it had proven a long ride home, even not accounting for the pursuit that no doubt followed me. Too late, now. Too late, with her inside walls none could breach. A rush of disbelief shot through me, left me vertiginous. I had ... succeeded?

Euphoria, elation, even in the dream.

The city at the end of the plain rose in successive tiers culminating in the royal palace, mountain-like. Such was Kêr-Ys, the greatest city in all the King-doms of Man. It was a gem upon the lowlands, seeming to rise from the sea itself in a wonder of architecture none could replicate. A spiralling path wound around the tiers, forced me to slow the mare to a walk. I patted the horse's neck in appreciation; the mare had striven to bring us home with such speed. She had earned her rest this night, and more besides.

Hanging lanterns, not yet lit, dangled overhead, strung from the fine-mortared walls of buildings framing narrow streets. Most of the structures we passed were cut from the same granite as the walls. The city would have been maze-like, I thought, had I not known it so well.

I knew this place! Not only in the dream, but I had seen it in life, in the waking world. I had swum through its inundated streets, darted beneath its crumbling archways, and delved the now-fractured buildings that had tumbled atop one another. But here, they stood whole, a wonder, a glory of Man. Houses were piled atop one another, shops beneath many, some glowing with candlelight.

A riot of smells wafted through the alleys, fresh bread—how did I know that?—mingling with the scent of refuse and gutter filth. In alleys smaller than even this street, I saw dishevelled vagabonds huddled beneath threadbare cloaks. I saw colonies of rats, their eyes glinting in their hiding holes. At inter-sections, I saw marble statues twice the height of a Man, clad in the fine raiment of kings.

One, a hammer-bearing statue at the heart of the lower levels, I paused at, bowed my head. Why did I do that? An acknowledgment, I thought, to the builder of this grand city.

Some townsfolk recognised me, gawked or genuflected.

"It's all right," I whispered into my sister's ear, for my voice seemed to soothe the babe. I hoped the child would never remember witnessing the murders. "Teutates allow you recall naught of this."

I continued my gradual ascent up the tiers, passing through archways that divided levels, where iron-banded gates could be thrown shut in the impossible chance of an assault breaching the city. Those hinges must have rusted, for never had the gates been sealed. At last, I crested onto the highest tier, one rimmed by buildings decorated with graven facades depicting dolphins or whales or sea life I knew so well. Above, the palace gleamed, for the golden trim worked into the stone caught the morning or evening light, turning the mountain summit into an aureate beacon. I could envisage it, uncertain how.

At the palace gates, I was met by more guards, one of which took the reins of my horse as I climbed down. "See Morvoren gets pampered like a queen," I said to the guard leading my mount toward the stables.

"You found her!" someone called, and I turned to see two young men scrambling over, one with red-blond hair, one darker, his locks almost black.

I knew them! I knew them, well, knew them in my heart. "Sétanta," I said, clasping arms with the auburn-haired youth. "Aye, I found her." A thrill shot up my arm at his touch. I wanted more, wanted his hands on my skin. Still, I forced myself to pull back, take the dark-haired one's arm. "Moccus," I said, nodding at him as well. The man squeezed my arm ere releasing me.

"We feared for you, Princess," Sétanta said.

I laid my palm along his cheek. "We've no need for fear now. All is settled, and Gwezenneg is sent to the Otherworld. Now, I restore my father's other child to him, and then, I think, comes the wine."

I CRAVED MORE of that world. Knowing myself for a fool, I swam back to the structure where I'd left Donall and took to spying on the people there. Three times I came to that shore, and three times did I eavesdrop upon those from the Kingdoms of Man.

On the first day, I saw two white-robed men escort another man to the shore. This man looked bedraggled, his beard and hair unkempt. Beneath his eyes welled shadows deep as lightless depths of the ocean. Despite his appearance, he held his head high and shoulders stiff with relentless pride. His robed escorts guided him down to the water until they stood with the waves lapping at their legs. The man, whom I now took to be their prisoner, refused to meet their gaze or to look at the sea, but rather stared at the sky.

"Aelfstan of Melusine," one of the robed men intoned with an air of ritual, "here beneath the Fane of Teutates do we consecrate your soul to the God who watches. May he witness this sacrifice and be appeased. May your body wash down to the Otherworld and thus sate the fearsome ire of those beyond. We honour your offering."

At last, the prisoner deigned to look at his executioners and he spat. "No offerings will earn you enough favour to save your faltering lands. Already, Nemedia gasps her last rattling breaths through decaying lungs."

Though the robed men muttered something, they did not further address this man, Aelfstan. Rather, when their invocations had finished, they seized him by both shoulders and drove him to his knees. Then they bent him over, holding his head beneath the tide.

I watched, fascinated and horrified at the display. Mistake me not, for merrows will deal with one another with far more brutality than that which I saw here. When facing another clan or a rival, my kind will claw and bite and tear to shreds those before us and then feast upon ruined flesh, and all this in the space of heartbeats. I think what unnerved me was not the death but rather the pretence of civility these men affected whilst murdering one of their fellows. A merrow would have said, hate when hate is warranted. Kill, when it so behoves you. But do so with honesty, for our pretexts are lies believed by none save, perhaps, our own selves. And what use to lie to ourselves?

On my second visit to the fane, I chanced to see Donall walking along the cliff above the shore. So I pulled myself up on the rocks just below the cliff, where he would have to peer directly down to spot me, and I listened. From my position I could not see him, either, but I heard shuffling footsteps draw nigh to where he paced, and I imagined him turn to meet the newcomer.

"You're Faoinèis," he said, his voice raspier than when I heard him on the ship. "They say you saved me."

What was this? *I* had saved him, and though I knew it absolved me of having broken the law if he had not seen and so I ought to have been relieved, still a flush of irritation coloured my cheeks at the thought he did not even know what I had done for him. What I, a merrow, had risked to save a mortal life. I began combing my fingers through my raven locks, imagining myself calling out to him and dazzling him with my lush hair, fine figure, and glistening tail. *Look here, upon my argent scales, son of Man! Are not they works of glory?* Such are the idle fancies we all have when we feel underappreciated.

"Aye, I suppose I did," a woman's voice said. "Or rather, I heard the voice of some goddess calling to me, bidding me to save you. Epona, perhaps, if she took exception to the Kelpie drowning men in her image. If you've a mind to offer thanks, offer it to her fane, when next you find one." The woman blew out a long breath. "So ... Now that you've cast aside Death's shadow, I don't mind saying you were a right bunch of fools, you were. What, did you never hear the legend of the Kelpie?"

Donall grunted, hesitating before he answered her. "Aye. We heard. We thought it a bard's tale woven to earn them an extra share of wine and maybe spread ... er. Their names."

"Oh, give over. Don't go thinking because I'm a druid I don't know what men want spread."

I smirked at that, struggling not to chortle and reveal myself. The man cleared his throat and, from the sound of it, shuffled about in the dirt hunting for something to say. I've seen Mererid like that, swishing her tail in the sand as if doing so might conjure forth some witticism.

"What were you doing, sailing these parts so nigh to the Corryvreckan? That hole drops straight down to the Otherworld, it does, and more fool you for coming within a league of it."

"A fool I am," Donall admitted. "And my fellows pay for it." They seemed to be walking away as this last was spoken, and I could make no more of their words.

On the third day, I watched as men and women came and went from the fane. At first, none drew close enough to the shore for me to hear them, and I could only wait and watch, seized by wonder. In the afternoon, one of the men from before, no longer robed in white, came to meet a visitor who landed a small ship on the shore. The newcomer hopped ashore and awaited the fane-keeper, who raised a hand in cautious greeting. "Hail," the keeper said.

"Hail. I am Sétanta, a knight out of Kêr-Ys." And I knew him, from my dream! Age had changed him, somewhat, added more muscle and more lines of care, but still he had that shock of fiery, curled hair. How was it possible a man I'd seen in my dream, a man I had never before laid eyes on, now stood before me in the flesh?

The keeper shifted in some discomfort. "Ill fortune, that."

"Aye," Sétanta agreed. "I search for the lost princess, and thus I'm resolved to consult every fane and oracle across Nemedia, if I must. Can you read the auguries?"

"You're two days late; our last prisoner of war went to the Otherworld the day before last, and I've none more to gut unless you offer your own bowels. But regardless, no divination I ever saw said a whit about that girl. The time for finding her is long past, and Nemedia is broken beyond repair."

I did not grasp the whole of his meaning, but his sentiment seemed an eerie mimicry of the doomed man's own accusations, as if these keepers knew well enough their sacrifices and efforts little availed them.

Nor could I say why, but on hearing about this lost princess, my soul ached with a pity I could not name. Had I not, in that other life, *saved* the princess? I had held her in my arms whilst greeting a much younger Sétanta. None of this made sense now, and the questions scalded me like jellyfish tendrils, venomous and burning. Disquieted, I slipped back into the waters and swam home.

Bodies without heads. And her, a sister, missing, lost. As if I would permit a knife to hover forever a hair above her throat.

My skin prickled and I rubbed my arms. It was not the chill of the night. I had the distinct sensation of gazes upon my back, watching me, waiting to see what I would do. If my courage would break. Almost, I could see two heads, one male, one female, gazing at me through the foliage. Spurring me on.

Bodies without heads. Heads without bodies. Souls without rest.

A haunting, damning refrain playing through my mind, teasing me with inchoate images on the fringes of my vision. Almost there, almost I saw them, watchful.

I knelt before the altar, smoothed the ashes in the stump's hollow. The wood was almost petrified. The centre had seen so many offerings made here, over years, over centuries. Another head, once, I had heard. I would not go that far. Prayed I never needed to go that far.

Some said Creiddylad had blessed this oak when it lived. A sacred nemeton, aye. The Earth thrummed with pain, here; in times, cruelty was warranted, sacrifice needful. I had learnt well, for I had always proved an apt.

I wedged my torch into the loam, then emptied my basket, spreading the rapunzel flowers across the offering bed. A breeze set the leaves soughing, had me casting about. I saw only the darkness, and it was vast, encroaching upon me like giant fingers closing. Ready to engulf me. Ready to welcome me into its gloom. A place prepared for me unless I turned back.

Bodies without heads.

My breath caught in my throat. I was choking, gasping, almost ready to break into weeping. Not again, not now. "I have not come for tears," I told myself. Leastwise, not my tears.

Blood for blood, and pain for pain.

I took up my torch, touched it to the flowers, watched them curl and char. Tendrils wafted skyward, vanished into the dark. "Black Annis, Black Annis ..." I chanted, struggling to keep my voice steady, struggling not to falter, given my rising panic. "'Neath a moonless night I call you. Black Annis, Black Annis, in the time of wolves I summon you. Black Annis, Black Annis, from the shadows come."

THE INTENSITY of my dream had grown and grown again, and I awakened to my own thrashing on my grotto floor. The wild spasms of my tail had overturned several of the artefacts I'd collected, including the marble statue from the ruins. I dashed over to it, inspecting every nook for further cracks, aghast at the thought I might have damaged so irreplaceable a piece of history. I found a small chip had broken off the hair, leaving a sharp edge which I could not stop myself from prodding at.

I did not know what the dream itself meant, but I think, had I the human ability to weep, I would have done so, for it left my soul aching with a longing I could not name. I could not shake the sense that these were *my* memories somehow, in some way beyond all sense of logic. Once, I thought myself bearing witness to the life of a mortal woman, the woman depicted by the statue. Now, though, I knew, with an intuition I could neither explain nor deny, I had somehow *been* that woman.

I looked deep into the green eyes of that statue, holding it in trembling hands, struggling even to form the words I knew I must say. "Am I you?" I knew that I was, knew it was all real.

Even waking, flickers of memory of another life flashed in my mind, inchoate and yet damningly real. I recall the thought, the fear, that, if madness had taken me, I might not recognise it. Still, even so, the statue wanted to speak to me of who she, of who *I*, had been.

When I told my grandmother this—for seeing me distraught, she took me for a long swim to the dolphin run, where we could watch a pod at play—she fell silent, staring at the moonlight filtering through the waves. It must have been a clear night above, for argent bands had turned the whole expanse of the sea into liquid silver. After a time, she sighed, bubbles spilling from her mouth. "It is true that in death fae souls are reborn into new bodies, and those who are strong may recall who once they had been. Rebirth may become but waking from a dream. But to have the memories of Man ... I cannot think it likely, Lí Ban."

Ahead, several dolphins swam closer, squeaking as if eager to draw us from our distress. They would not come too nigh, of course, for they could sense something perilous about our natures. But their kind tended to watch merrows, and I oft wondered what went through their minds when they looked upon us.

"Not likely," I said, "does not mean impossible. Can you prove it could not have happened?"

Grandmother scowled. "If you spent less time lost in fancy and more attending to your lessons you might recall the burden of proof for an existential claim lies on the one making it. As no fae—yes, no *other* fae, fine—recalls a human life, it stands to reason that either such memories are sucked away by the Lethe, or else no such rebirths occur. Either way, you cannot produce evidence of your theory, meaning placing belief in it is logically unfounded."

"And my dreams?" I protested, for they were achingly real to me, even if I alone of all the fae in the World had experienced such.

Her frown became sympathetic. "You've spent your life obsessed with Man. The mind can produce sensations with no reality outside of its own sphere, and that truth, Lí Ban, we *have* been able to verify. So is it a wonder that you should dream of yourself in these fancies?" She was right, of course. And still, her answer left me unsatisfied.

They say Nudd shattered the Tower of Glass, though it cost him his life, and in so doing denied our clan the ability to ever again walk on land. Thus did the fomorii rulers of Inis Fáil become the merrows who would never again leave our refuge of Cantref Gwaelod. Perhaps Nudd and his ilk had thus cursed my kind. But the power to take human form had existed once in days long gone.

I knew in my heart the truth—I had been the green-eyed woman, the princess of Kêr-Ys—and I knew, too, I must have my answers about whatever had unfolded in my past life. Something in all this called to me, beckoned me as surely as the siren song of the Voice could have called Men to their dooms. So even knowing the peril, knowing there was a chance I had lost my mind, went now to my doom, I could not turn back.

INTERLUDE: DAHUT

What had she done? That thought paraded through Dahut's mind in endless refrain, damning and insistent. All the years she'd spent in druidic training, all the countless hours spent memorising the vast lore of her people—she had thought it made her wise. She had thought she could call upon forces that someone like Gwezenneg could scarce fathom. But all that time, Aodh had warned her against bargaining with the Otherworld.

And she had done it anyway.

She had called for Black Annis, the red-hooded hag, even knowing all the fearsome tales of the being. Mothers threatened intractable children with her, said she would come for them in the night and gnaw on their bones. Bards claimed, any fool enough to venture outside after dusk might hear her grinding her teeth in the boughs of a tree, and then the only chance was to flee home, never once looking back. She'd heard tale the Other could flense off a man's skin in seven heartbeats, using bronze claws that grew from her hands.

But Dahut had known better than that. There were no claws or sharpened teeth, just a being from beyond the Mortal Realm, her form slight as a young girl, hidden beneath a red riding hood. Girl-like, perhaps, but an Elder creature, possessed of lore unknown to Man, one who could help her. Who could grant her vengeance and allow her to save her infant sister.

Dahut paced around the palace terrace, hands flexing at her side, jaw working furiously. Up here, Father had commissioned statues of them all: himself, Mother, and Dahut. One day, there would have been a statue for her baby sister. Would have, had Dahut not lost her a second time. Each statue was carved and painted by the finest artist in the kingdom, rendered in lifelike detail, from the flaxen shade of Mother's hair to the vibrant green of Dahut's eyes, to Father's well-oiled moustache. Perfect flattery now seemed a perfect mockery.

Dahut had shed her vomit-soaked dress and donned a new one, darker green this time.

"Princess," Moccus ventured. She had summoned him and Sétanta, and for a time, they stood silent, waiting for her to address them. She knew they had not slept, for like everyone else, they had spent the night and all morn searching for the lost babe. Moccus was as young as his companion but exploding with muscles that made him look like he could rip Black Annis in half, should he chance to find the Other. Dahut had seen Moccus at the feast, devouring five servings of boar and an equal amount of wine from the provinces. If his indulgences then slowed him now, he gave no sign of it.

Sétanta wasn't looking at either of them. The other knight stood at the balustrade, peering out over the city as if he might look through the granite walls and spot the babe hidden there. As if, with keen enough senses, he could find someone wherever they were secreted away. Many of her father's other knights continued searching the city and some had moved on to nearby villages. She doubted they would find the girl.

"It's plain enough Black Annis took her beyond the walls," Dahut said after a moment. "The Other would not linger here, at the heart of the greatest city of Man. We may pray she yet lingers in Nemedia ..." Dahut did not want to countenance the idea the girl had been taken to Falias, the city of the Sluagh, one of the four cities of Dark Faerie. Druidic lore claimed they did that, sometimes—took children. But in such cases, they left behind changelings in facsimile of the stolen babe, and Black Annis had left naught behind save grief. Or would she have left a changeling had Dahut not interrupted her? She couldn't know. It was hard to swallow. "Even if she remains in Nemedia, the kingdom is vast."

Now, Sétanta turned to look at her, grim faced. "Should she make for the very Hinterlands of Falias, still we shall pursue. In such a case as this, the borders of the kingdom mean no more to us than they do to the winds. We will find her, Princess."

Dahut bowed her head in acknowledgment, scarce trusting herself to speak. Every breath scorched her throat with acid grief. Her gut ached from the roil of it. "Go," she rasped. "Return only with my sister." And when they had departed, she collapsed against the balustrade, choking down a scream.

If she had not called upon the red-hooded hag, she could never have recovered her sister in the first place. Yet in doing so, she had perhaps damned the girl to worse fate still. Why would Black Annis want a daughter of Man? Surely not ... surely the tales of her eating infants could not be truth. Parents threatened children with such to bring them in line, not because anyone thought it really happened. No, no. For why would the Other bother bargaining and using her dark powers to aid Dahut, when she could have stolen a meal from any home in Nemedia? From Starfall Vale, which abutted the Hinterlands?

Shattered, Dahut pushed off the balustrade. The knights would hunt their way, but Dahut must follow her own path. Some druids had gifts that allowed them to intuit things, to know things others could never understand. Dahut had no such abilities, but she would find those who did and beseech their help. She must do so; her sister depended on her. The kingdom depended on her.

IN A NEMETON, a sacred grove, Dahut met with the chief druid, Donn, and Elouan, who sat in meditation. Moonlight filtered through the leaves overhead, casting bands of illumination through the grove, letting it seem blessed. Once, this place would have allowed Dahut peace, where she could commune with the gods and try to sense the will of the spirits of land and water. One tale claimed that Nemed himself, the founder of Nemedia and her line as the father of Gofannon, was named for the nemetons. This grove was dedicated to Epona, the Horse

Goddess. Her children ran in the plains beyond here and the woodlands, untamed and wild.

Restlessness made Dahut's skin itch and she could not stop fidgeting and pacing about the grove. The peace of this place no longer reached her heart. It could not pierce the mass of nerves that had become her flesh. It could not burrow through the scars upon her soul.

Donn followed her with his eyes, his gaze ordering her to stillness, though she found such impossible. They said Elouan could leave his body behind, walk in the Otherworld. If her pacing distracted the druid on his spirit journey, he might lose himself. She had heard that, in the Realms beyond the Mortal, Elouan could take the form of a horse and run through sidereal spaces to seek answers. She had seen him ingest entheogenic mushrooms before falling into the trance, which left her to wonder whether his spirit really took on forms or he merely perceived it. Or whether there was, in fact, a difference.

The chief druid stepped up to her, caught her wrist, and yanked her to a stop. "'Tis not your fault." His voice was a whisper.

That was, of course, a lie. Dahut had made her choices because she wanted Gwezenneg to suffer. She wanted him to pay for his treachery. The subject king had broken his oath of fealty, had murdered her mother and sister, had held a child hostage. How could she not wish harm upon him for such crimes? And Father had sought to negotiate, to wait. To bide his time, as if the situation might resolve itself with patience. Such reticence had inflamed Dahut. If the king would not act to protect his family, she had to do so. Had she mistaken his thoughtful repose for weakness? If so, it was the same mistake the subject kings made. And now, with the princess gone again, King Gralon had retreated further into the labyrinth of his own thoughts, and Kêr-Ys looked weaker than ever. More than two dozen petty kings ruled Nemedia in his name. How many had begun to question whether they could not hold their own kingdom, apart from Nemedia?

After all, the other Kingdoms of Man had also once been part of Nemedia. Nemed and his children had settled all civilised lands of the continent of Golgleth, and their legacy ought to have endured so long as Men walked upon the Earth. But the sons of Nemed, demigods though they were, faded. The Black Forest, once ruled by Owain, in the years after he left Bro Érech, broke away without his leadership. Then came the kingdoms of Lakenwald and Starfall Vale and the Willows. For a time, five Kingdoms of Man flourished. A time, only. For Falias stretched out its hand and the Sluagh wiped away the Willows. The rural kingdom of the north fell to the Wild Hunt. Night after night, so druidic stories told, the skies would crackle with thunder and fell laughter, and foul things would stalk the darkness. Until, in the end, no Men yet remained in the Willows, and it became a twisted place known as the Hinterlands of Falias. Some said, even, that Gwyn ap Nudd himself rode at their head, deathless and craving.

And Dahut had known, even then, Black Annis was an Other, possibly even a Sluagh of Falias. She had known these ancient beings were capable of malice and unfathomable motive, had been warned by Aodh, and still she had turned to one. For what choice had she had?

"Not your fault," Donn repeated, seeming to follow her thoughts, though she had not spoken. "All we can do is what seems best with the knowledge we have at the time. It would be vanity to think we can know all things."

Dahut looked to him, met his gaze. "It was vanity. I didn't make my choice only to save my missing sister. I sought vengeance."

"All Men revenge wrongs done unto them and theirs. Such has always been the way of the World, Dahut. If you cared so little as to take no pride in your kin, would that not prove more blameworthy?"

Did he believe his words, or did he try to assuage her guilt because his training had allowed her to call on Black Annis in the first place? "I bargained with a creature ages older than myself and thought somehow I would come out ahead. What would you name that, save vanity?"

"Desperation." That, she could not deny. Desperation was both the knife in one's belly and the blade in one's hand. It stole reason with its agonies even as it armed one with the willingness to go places one would not have otherwise dared. Few foes could prove more dangerous than the desperate.

A wolf's howl rent the night, an echo of her melancholy.

After a time, Donn released his grip on her arm. "The children of Nemed fought so bravely for these lands ... So bravely, only to fall one by one. And like them, the Kingdoms of Man begin to falter."

Aye, Owain, Gofannon, Gwyn, the others, all gone now. And Dahut, her sister, they were the last of the line of Nemed. If the subject kings took this opportunity to break away from the rule of Kêr-Ys, the lands of Man would become further fractured. A swell of emotion choked her, made it hard to form her next words. "I will not see Nemedia follow the Willows into the night."

"Gofannon entrusted your line with the Celestial Jewel, handed down from lost Tianxia. It is the jewel that wrought the glory of Kêr-Ys in lowlands reclaimed from the sea. His divine blood runs through your veins, Dahut. You can yet be the beacon of light that reunites Man, but you must be strong to do so. You must show them all you are strong. Be the Whirlwind, Aveldro, and sweep away your opposition."

She bit her lip. His words bowed her shoulders, a fresh strain, as if finding her sister were not obligation enough. "My father ..."

"Is a wise and thoughtful man. But you, Princess, are cast from the mould of the Smith Lord himself, and there is iron in you."

Was there? Dahut straightened herself and looked back to Elouan who had begun to stir from his trance. "I will find my sister. All else shall keep until *that* is done."

The other druid moaned and leant forward onto his elbows, head down to the ground. Dahut took two steps toward him before a tremendous belch burst from the other druid's lips. Then she was at his side, hand on his back as he groaned, clutching his guts. "What happened?" she asked.

"Feels like rats gnawing inside my bowels ..."

She shivered at the mental image. A price, always, came due. To touch the world beyond our own, it took a hefty toll on body, on mind. "How can we aid you?"

He didn't look up. "None of those I consulted believe she was taken to Falias. They said ... Black Annis is a title. But they either did not know or would not reveal the true name of that Sluagh." So she was a Sluagh. But if she had not taken the child to the Sluagh city, where had the hag hidden her sister?

"What else?"

"She lingers in the Kingdoms of Man, though to what end or where, I could not gather. I'm sorry, Princess, I couldn't ..." Another belch, and then he curled over onto his side. Even in the moonlight, she could see the sheen of sweat slicking his neck. Shivers wracked him.

Dahut stood and looked to Donn. "I'll tend to him," the chief druid said.

A breeze rustled through the nemeton, setting the branches soughing and ruffling Dahut's hair and dress. "I need to get word to the knights." If her sister was still in the Kingdoms of Man, hope remained.

Hope and desperation, for Dahut must find her before Black Annis made whatever use of the girl she intended. Time had run short.

PART II

Such it was that, in the days ere the rise of Man, did the Elder Races war betwixt themselves. Like the shifting of tides did each side ebb and flow. And the blood of giants and fae ran in rivers across the land. And the Earth and the waters wept for sorrow, to see their children come to such internecion.
*   —Annals of Findias, history of the Tylwyth Teg*

2

———

I could see but one path to attain my goal, for I knew of only one being that might possess the power to let me walk on land and live among the humans. Primal dread bid me turn back. Of course, and I considered doing so with each league I drew closer to the Corryvreckan. Fear slithered over me, a skulking eel, ready to lunge. Since my youngest days, my sisters and I were warned that this place, beneath the North Sea, was forbidden to us. Only those laden with sacrifice or tribute dared approach the lair of the Kelpie. If they asked for aught, it would be to petition to pass back and forth to Faerie. No one, so far as I knew, had ever called upon the ancient spirit and bid it turn its powers to personal use.

Such was madness. Such was vanity. Such was the pull of my heart.

Fields of twisted coral polyps grew around the approach, bent by the pull of churning waters. It struck me, even life was warped by the nearness to the Otherworld. I pushed onward, trying not to imagine the creatures as writhing in pain.

The subsea currents grew wild as I drew nigh, tugging at my hair, threatening to yank me into the churning waters of the maelstrom. Only by keeping low could I stay my course. The seabed was cracked, as though blasted apart by some colossal explosion, with sulphuric vents spewing toxic vapours in blinding clouds. Crevasses pitched away into unknown depths, from some of which billowed the red-tinged incandescence of the fires of the Earth. Swimming over these, my tail was scalded with heat that, had I lingered, might have boiled me alive.

At last, I came to the Kelpie's palace. I had never laid eyes upon the place, but I knew it could be no other, though it was not so much a structure as a cavern. Shards of rock akin to gigantic steepled fingers shot out over a crater beneath the eye of the maelstrom. Amid those rock lances sat a cavernous opening, like the maw of a behemoth. Storytellers among us told legends of the great dragons of the deep. In tales, some were legged monstrosities that would swim or crawl along the seafloor, whist others had serpentine bodies framed with savage spines and horns. Though I saw no evidence of a skeleton, the cavern's mouth reminded me of the skull of such a draconic beast.

If the Kelpie were to have a palace, I could think of no more fitting place for it. I had come all this way with clear purpose ... Still, heart hammering and gut roiling, I hesitated. The spirit, I knew, must already sense my presence. If it wished, it could devour me, body and soul, and should I vex it with my trespass, that now seemed a probable outcome to this whole endeavour. What a fool I had been to think I could bargain with the hoary incarnations of the sea itself.

I lingered there, knowing I must flee, yet unable to stomach the thought of abandoning my aim. For that must be the consequence of my turning back now; if I gave up here, I gave up for good and all. I would have admitted, even to myself, that my studies into Man, my dreams of a past life, all of it, were but childish fancy. I could have cast them aside, taken a mate as Father suggested, and reared spawn. I could have settled into my life as the stars had laid it out before me, and one day, resigned to my Fate, all this would seem but a faded memory.

But why should I care what the stars had ordained for me? I wanted my life, and I needed to live it on my own terms or not at all. What matter if I perished if the alternative was the slow smothering of who and what I was?

I swallowed my fear and darted forward, racing toward that cavernous maw before my courage could fail me. Faster I sped, eyes half closed lest I gaze upon something else to quicken the gnawing dread in my gut.

Then I was within that cave and gawping at what I saw. The eerie red light of the crevasses filled this space, rising from vents in the floor, and glittering off what must have been thousands of years of offerings. Beads of pearls ran in endless chains about a space almost as wide as Father's whole palace. Piles of metal discs—bronze and gold—lay scattered. Amid them glinted garnets and fluorite and quartz and great chunks of amber as big as my torso. There were Man-made instruments of silver; some of these I took for decorative weapons or tools, though many I could not identify, no matter how long I stared at them. I saw a bejewelled bronze cap that was, perhaps, intended to protect one's skull. Too, there were crafts of iron, encrusted with rust. Were these all offerings made over the course of millennia? Thousands of years of Men trying to propitiate a spirit, even as merrows too did so.

Surely, a spirit of the water had no use for the treasures of Man. Did the Kelpie collect them merely for the obeisance they represented? Did it relish the act of worship for its own sake? It left me wondering if the spirit had any more use for the bodies and souls my kind offered it than it did for the baubles thrown into the depths by humans. I did not have longer to ponder that, however, for the water began to churn, yanking on my hair and body. I turned, and a spiralling lance broken off the greater maelstrom burst into the cavern. It touched down not far from where I swam, and I darted to one side, arms raised in warding, shark-teeth out before I knew what I was doing. The spiral turned into its own miniature whirlpool before coalescing into a creature of Man-like shape. Its onyx hair, as long as mine, billowed about it like each lock had a mind of its own, a nest of eels wriggling in the dark. The creature was heavily muscled, but it sat at ease upon a throne of rock. I was drawn to its eyes, for they seemed pools of liquid darkness and I could not look away. With one finger, it beckoned me and despite my fear, I scrambled over to quiver before the Kelpie.

"What would you have, little mermaid?" the Kelpie demanded, his voice booming through his palace and inside my skull. It was everywhere and everything, and I was suffused with a power beyond my ken. Small wonder mortals and fae alike would choose to offer aught we had for the favour of this entity—his wrath seemed a thing we dare not imagine.

I swallowed, struggling not to grovel. "Human legs, to walk among Mankind as my ancestors once did."

"The fomorii lost their war. To dwell forever beneath the sea is the curse levelled upon you when Lugus slew Balor One-Eyed. And you would have me lift that curse?" His mirth saturated the waters with malevolence, as if the whole cavern threatened to break into terrible violence if given but the slightest push.

"I do not speak for the whole of my clan," I protested. "I cannot account for deeds done long before my birth, though I imagine both sides wrought glory and woe in equal measure. Let the past lie only in story. I ask only for the power to go myself. I ... I have to know."

"What you have lost in lives gone by?"

I rocked back, the Kelpie having all but confirmed my intuitions that I had once lived as a mortal. Aye, I had been the green-eyed woman of the statue. Had lived, had died, and been born again. Not daring to speak, I managed a timid nod. Perhaps the ancient spirit thought me a fool, but between relief at his implication, and fear, and anticipation, I was rendered speechless.

The Kelpie chuckled, the sound dark, damning. "And you give not a whit for what you might have gained." Though I did not understand his words, they left me uneasy. "But aye, you come to me nigh to the equinox, when the worlds balance, and great deeds might be done. But for a price, little mermaid, ever for a price. I can brew for you a tonic that will grant you human form, though even that shall cost you, for once you take it, you shan't again swim with that beautiful tail nor breathe beneath the sea through your gills. This world of the deep will be forevermore denied to you. Such is the trade you must make to gain access to the surface. And more, though you shall dance upon beautiful legs, and walk with grace, every step shall feel as though blades slice your dainty feet."

After steadying myself, I rose to face him, jaw firm. "Such is my burden. Where comes your price, Lord?"

"Two things. The first, the source of your power shall be mine. I shall cut from your mouth your pretty little tongue and, with it, take the Voice."

I blanched, aghast the spirit could even imagine such a horrid thing. Perhaps he could devour the organ and enhance his own might, but the very idea of cutting the tongue from a living person was obscene. Already, I trembled from anticipation of the pain. I wondered if he would have let me flee at that point. I imagined myself darting away, though I could see him seizing me by hands or currents of the sea and holding me as his prisoner. Still, even if I could have escaped, I would not have chosen it. If you have never known desire, never felt the pull of a purpose beyond life itself, perhaps you cannot understand the willingness to sacrifice everything to follow it through. "Second?" I rasped, fearing it would be the last word I ever spoke.

The Kelpie leant forward, and, though his eyes remained pitch black, I swear I saw a malicious glint within them. "*You*, mermaid, stole one of my prizes from me. For that temerity, I shall have your fate tied to his. You took a soul that would have been mine, so unless he binds his soul to yours, unless you win his heart, your soul shall take his place. Should this man you pilfered ever promise the binding of his soul to another, you will perish and be drawn back here in death. Mine."

He spoke, nigh as I could tell, of the human custom of making oaths of lifetime mating. I knew, then, I had fallen into a terrible trap. He had known me from the first moment, perhaps had always known why I had come here, and had thus prepared a fitting punishment. As the Kelpie saw it, I had wronged him; affronted his momentous pride. For that crime, I must be made to suffer. And so, too, I realised there had never been any backing out of this. If I would have demurred, he'd have killed me, I have little doubt. I think, perhaps, even without that, I would have made the same choice, but who can say such things? We can never really know what we would do in situations other than those we face, and I was there, in the seat of his power, and forced to take the only bargain he offered. It was a chance, not only to live but to gain everything I had ever wanted.

"I accept," I said, because I could not have said aught else.

"Then come forth, mermaid, and stick out your tongue."

Quivering with terror, I did so. The Kelpie grasped a silver blade with one hand and with the other seized my tongue in a grip strong as rock. I cannot describe to you the waves of agony that overcame me when he cut it from my mouth. Any attempt I made to put such things into words would prove crass and, in any case, fall far short of the trauma of the event.

I scarce recall what happened next, so overcome was I by the pain and loss and fear and horror of it all. I wound up lying on the beach, and there was a bottle in my hand. My mouth was filled with the salty, metallic taste of my blood, and it sparked a feverish desire to tear into a foe and savage them. But there was no one to accost, and anyway, I had brought this on myself. So I broke the stopper and chugged the draught in a single swig, no doubt swallowing a stomachful of blood in the process. I remember hurling the empty phial out into the sea and watching it drift, thinking maybe the current would pull it back to the Corryvreckan and down to the Kelpie.

I did not watch long, however, for a horrific cramp built in my gut. It spread lower, pooling in the opening between my pelvic fins. Razors seemed to flense across my flesh, then carve deeper, gutting me from my nethers downward. Delirium took me, and perhaps unconsciousness became a mercy. I felt myself ripped in twain, and then, I felt no more.

Leaves rustled behind me; bushes disturbed. I leapt to my feet. Spun. There, amid the undergrowth, she stood, a bare silhouette in the darkness and shrouded by a blood-red cloak. She was a little woman, much shorter than me, and yet her presence filled the grove. Something vast. Something ... monstrous in scope. Like seeing a protruding root and knowing you saw only a tiny vestige of the whole.

"What would you have?" the Other asked.

No turning back. Never any turning back. Heads without bodies. A missing babe. "Vengeance. I want to see Gwezenneg brought low for all he has done. I want to see him writhe in agony before he dies. I want to bring my sister home, alive and safe."

"I will have your treasure."

A price, always, of course. Well, let her empty our coffers, if it please her. What matter silver or gold next to blood? "As much as you can carry," I assured her.

From within her red cloak, the Other produced a phial, held it out to me. No claws, despite the tales. Just fingers, just a tiny hand, as of a girl. "Drink, before you get to him. All his deep cunning shall be overshadowed beneath the rising mountain of his lust." Not what I had wished for, but it would do. It meant that I would look into his eyes as I killed him. I said that, said I wanted to see him brought low. In her other hand, she offered a second phial. "When it is done, drink this one, and eyes shall slide over you, like water flowing around river stones. You will walk free from his castle."

I AWAKENED to the harsh light of the sun in my eyes. Its punishing rays had turned my skin a vibrant pink that stung to the touch and left me feeling queasy. Nevertheless, as the Kelpie had promised, I now had smooth human legs where my scales and tail had always been before. Too, I found my genitals changed and rather foreign. I rubbed my neck and realised my gills were gone. As were my shark-teeth and the nictitating membranes of my eyes. Was I mortal? If any trace of Faerie remained to me, it was a distant thing.

I hobbled to my feet, then moaned at the agony that shot through them. It was as if I had dragged my raw flesh across coarse stones. The pain sent me tumbling back onto the sand, and there, for the first time, I wept. Hot tears spilled from my eyes, as if I needed further confirmation that all I had been had changed forever. Was this not what I had wished for? I had gone seeking this bargain, had agreed to it. It meant I had little right to complain of it now, even could I have given voice to my grief. Since I would never be able to express it to any living person, I resolved, then and there, I would bear it with a smile. If I could not tell what I suffered, then no one would ever know of my suffering. This, I told myself, would ward my heart against letting anguish consume me.

I knew that Mankind favoured garments, but I had none, so naked I walked along the beach, wincing with each step. The wind chilled my burnt flesh. I thought the cooling would have helped, but it only stung all the more. I was used to the currents billowing my hair around me; the winds, however, tossed it in wild gyrations that somehow managed to fly into my eyes no matter how I turned my head. There would, it seemed, prove a great many things about living as a mortal I would need to learn in very short order.

Among those, it seemed I no longer had my merrow tolerance for the cold, or at least that resistance had dwindled, for the breeze left me shivering. Bumps rose along my skin, and I gasped in shock whenever the wind grew strong.

I followed the shoreline, for I had no idea where I ought to be heading. Despite the pain in my feet, the discomfort of my body, my heart leapt at the landscape before me. The way the lapping of waves on the beach seemed to massage my raw nerves, even as the scent of clean brine helped orient me. Overhead, birds—gulls, I thought—squawked and soared, dropping on occasion to swoop down on a fish or crab. Here, I had found the world I had longed for, and learnt, whilst it was indeed alien, still I had tethers to what I had known.

But then, there were trees, soughing in a breeze, a sound I had never been close enough to land to hear ere now, at least whilst awake. Pale green leaves burst from its upper reaches, each a riot of colour, rich with life. Almost afraid, I edged away from the shoreline until I could lay my palm upon the surface of the tree's shaft. It lacked the pliant wetness of the ship I had touched and was rough, almost painfully so as I drew my hand along it. I had thought Men built their ships from trees, but perhaps I had been mistaken in that.

Reluctantly, knowing I could not find the answers I sought from a plant, no matter how fascinating, I made way back to the shore and continued onward. In my fancies, I had imagined Men rushing to embrace me into their midst with welcoming arms. I found, however, that a great deal of the surface world held no Men at all. Rather was populated by a plethora of strange plants and with birds and beasts that cast curious glances my way, leaving me to wonder if they imagined how I might taste. If so, they did not choose to try their luck, and I was grateful for that. I knew naught of human arts of war, though I fancied myself a competent hunter. Merrows had stronger bodies than mortals, needful to survive life under the sea, and I dared hope I retained at least that much of my origin. Still, I did not wish to put my strength to the test.

The land was not all flat, especially beyond the beach. For a time, I ogled the rolling, wavelike shapes of the Earth, rising and falling. Once, beneath the sea, I had listened whilst Grandmother berated Men for thinking the land forever unchanging. But here, seeing the shape of it, unflowing and frozen, I could see why Men would believe such a thing. I could imagine, without the sea to abrade the rising ground, those mounds might endure for eternity.

Along the hills, along the path up to them, tiny shoots of plant-life sprang up, most shorter than my forearm. Minuscule trees? Curious, I paced close and knelt beside a patch. With a trembling finger, I reached out and poked one of the leaf-like shoots. It was soft, smooth, perhaps a little sticky, and bent with almost no pressure applied. Content the creature could not harm me, I brushed a hand through the numerous blades of it. It was, I decided, akin to seagrass, albeit rougher for being dry.

I rose, pushed on. After walking long enough I learnt to trudge without grimacing, growing accustomed to the pain if not inured to it, I heard singing in the distance. The voice was feminine and pleasant, and though none in Cantref Gwaelod would have accounted her of much talent, my heart fair leapt at the sound of her voice. The song echoed off the hills and led me inland to where I found a wooden house, topped by a slanted surface upon which grew short grass, making the whole place look like another hill. In front of the home, a girl some years younger than myself sat in the dirt, gardening, even as I had once done, though I knew none of the plants she tended.

I tried to cry out for her but managed only a moan. She did not look up from her work. I waved at her, but of course she did not notice. At last, not knowing what to do, I trudged closer until the sound of my shuffling footfalls alerted her. The girl looked up, her eyes widening at my appearance.

"Ma!" the girl shrieked.

"What?" came the terse answering cry from within the house.

"There's a lass here."

"Don't need no lasses," the mother retorted. "Let me know when you find yourself a man, and we'll be talking."

"Uh ... Ma, she's got nary a stitch on and a bloody lip all telling a tale of its own ..."

Bloody lip? I wiped my face and found the wound from my mouth had left a dark crust, almost as if it had scabbed, though not on the injury. At least *that* no longer ached, so perhaps the Kelpie's tonic had staunched the bleeding as it transformed the rest of me.

"What the ...?" the mother now muttered, then gasped as she came out into the threshold of her doorway. I wanted to see around her, to see the dwelling, but her frame filled the space, and all I could make out was a warm gleam behind her. The woman wore a strip of fabric over her shoulders, perhaps for warmth, and after gawping for a moment, raced toward me. In an instant, she took that fabric and wrapt it around my shoulders and begun ushering me into her home. The place was the size of my grotto, smaller even, but so very warm. The heat radiated from a pit in the centre of the house where blazed what I recognised as a fire, though I had never chanced to draw nigh to one before. I stared at it, so enraptured by the strangeness of this thing pulsing with warmth—maybe too much warmth—I could not tear my gaze away even to examine the contents of the house. The flame danced as if alive, as if pulled by the currents of the sea, though even I knew fire could not survive underwater.

"What happened to you, lass?" the woman asked, drawing me to sit beside the fire. I wanted to tell her. At that moment, I wanted, maybe more than aught in the World, to confide in another person all I had endured and all I had experienced. I wanted to share my wonder, to ask my thousand, thousand questions. Being unable to do so rankled, irritating as having my tail chafed. How was I to live without being able to speak? Not knowing what else to do, I opened my mouth to show my missing tongue. She blanched but recovered quickly. "Taranis blast whoever did that to you! Well, let it not be said I'd turn away a woman in need. I'm Cora. Old Widow Cora they call me in town, though I'm not so old as all that, mind. Aye, the last man who said it to me face probably still has a lump beside his ear. So, then, first we'll be needing some clothes. Then I think a hot soup wouldn't be amiss from the look of you."

I did not know what soup was, so all I could do was shrug. Cora barked orders at her daughter, who returned with a long, coarse garment of green. The girl helped me don the raiment, at which point it took almost all my willpower to keep from scratching at everywhere it touched my skin. This thing itched and chafed and abraded and stank. I wondered if they had rendered it out of grass, for it had a similar colour.

Cora, meanwhile, set a large bowl-like object over the fire. The container was iron, and I shied away from it. I did not know, of a certain, that I retained my fae allergy to iron, but I had little desire to chance it. In the thing, murky water soon bubbled with the heat. I found the smell that emanated from the container not unpleasant. Curious, as much about the flame itself as the container, I reached for it.

The woman caught up my hand. "Famished are we, then? Still best you wait a wee bit." I sulked at that, frustrated she would not let me stick my fingers in the fire to examine its silky texture. I am not certain Cora noticed, and a few moments later, she scooped some of the bubbling water into a bowl. One, thankfully, made from wood, not iron. "'Tis fish soup."

She handed it to me, but I almost dropped it, shocked at the heat that seeped through the surface. But no, that too, was not unpleasant, I soon decided, and resolved if touching the warm bowl was so pleasant, I must needs touch the fire when she wasn't looking. I watched Cora's daughter serve herself another bowl, heft it to her lips, and drink. In parts of the sea, where magma runs close to the surface, vents can set the waters boiling. I could not imagine wanting to drink such waters, but these people seemed to think it mundane. Gingerly, I mimicked her gesture. The warmth filled my mouth, became a shock of pain in the place where the Kelpie had cut out my tongue. Tears welled in my eyes and I struggled to swallow. I set the bowl down, squeezed my eyes shut and willed the tears away.

Cora murmured concern. "Aye, that must ache something terrible, it must." These people were caring for me, saving me. My father always warned of the dangers of Men, and yet, huddled by the luxurious warmth of a fire, being fed, I could not imagine more gracious hosts. The woman had given me clothes, even if I found them itchy and restrictive and unnecessary.

How could I reject their hospitality? Besides, if I could not eat, I would perish. Setting my resolve, I picked up the bowl once more, took a small sip. By the time I had finished half the dish, I realised I still had hints of taste. I would not have expected to be able to taste aught, though perhaps enough remained of the root of my tongue. Was the dampened sensation a blessing, or would it only serve to remind me of a sense I had *almost* lost?

❧

ONCE MY BELLY was full of soup—which turned out quite pleasant, I decided—Cora draped another piece of fabric over my shoulders and bade me recline by the fire. It had not taken long for sleep to claim me once more. I dreamt once again of a soaring city and thought it now perhaps the very sunken ruin I'd oft visited on my search for artefacts.

I awakened to the sound of the woman speaking softly to her daughter.

"We've scarce the food to last ourselves," Cora told the girl. "There's naught for it save to see the poor dear to the chief. He'll make certain of a roof over her head and food in her belly."

Her daughter huffed. "A foundling girl? Mostlike she'll wind up a slave, and you know it."

"I know naught of the sort, and neither do you. Maybe they'll be finding her people. Maybe they can't but might still be needing a scullion or a maid. Any of it is better than her out on her own. Grows colder by the day, now."

"Does," the girl admitted.

I lay there, beside the crackling fire, and wondered what my future would hold. Part of me would be sad to leave this home, though even if they could have kept me, I could not have lingered here long. Because of the Kelpie's curse, I needed to find Donall, but I had no idea how to ask without my tongue. And Cora was right—I could not fend for myself in this new world. I remained at the mercy of others, hoping they would prove as kind as this woman and her daughter.

When I thought they slept, I wriggled over toward the fire pit and reached a finger into it. I expected to be able to grab a wisp of flame, but it lashed me like a jellyfish tendril and I sucked a sharp breath, shocked at the sensation.

"Ack," Cora said, noticing. "Get you back to sleep, lass."

A WOLF'S HOWL, sundering the night, in echo of my dark mood. I stood in a grove with two other men. One set in repose, eyes closed, seeming in a trance. The other stood by my side, his hand upon my bicep. He released me, spoke. "The children of Nemed fought so bravely for these lands ... So bravely, only to fall one by one. And like them, the Kingdoms of Man begin to falter."

Emotion rose in my breast, wavelike, almost enough to swallow my answer. "I will not see Nemedia follow the Willows into the night."

"Gofannon entrusted your line with the Celestial Jewel, handed down from lost Tianxia. It is the jewel that wrought the glory of Kêr-Ys in lowlands reclaimed from the sea. His divine blood runs through your veins, Dahut. You can yet be the beacon of light that reunites Man, but you must be strong to do

so. You must show them all you are strong. Be the Whirlwind, Aveldro, once again, and sweep away your opposition."

I bit my lip, felt the weight of his words bowing my shoulders. "My father ..."

"Is a wise and thoughtful man. But you, Princess, are cast from the mould of the Smith Lord himself, and there is iron in you."

I straightened, looking back to the trancing man. Felt my resolve turn to granite. "I will find my sister. All else shall keep until that is done."

❦

"'Tis but a short jaunt to Dùn Beinn," Cora assured me in the morn, perhaps mistaking my weariness for trepidation. Rather, I had not yet adapted to human diurnal schedules, though I was certain I would, given time. However, after we broke our fast on mushrooms and tomatoes, I decided Cora's estimation of a short jaunt differed from mine, perhaps because every step to her did not feel like dragging her feet along the desiccated remnants of coral.

Dahut, that man in my dream had called me, and I knew then who I had been in another life. Dahut, a princess of Kêr-Ys, a city taken by the waves. I wished I could inquire for more details from Cora, but I had no means to give voice to my myriad questions, and so they swelled inside me until the pressure made me feel apt to burst at the seams.

We passed over hills bedecked with rocky protrusions, following an ill-defined path through land that seemed harsh and threatening to me. I could not help but imagine swimming over all of this, though I strove not to grow bitter with such thoughts and forced a smile to my face whenever Cora glanced back at me. Trees of many kinds dappled the hills, but I did not know the names of any of them, and I had no way to ask. Perhaps, even if I could have, Cora might have thought me mad or a fool, not knowing such things at my age.

I saw tiny rocks all along the path. Some skittered away from my feet —Cora had given me worn-down foot coverings—and bounced delightfully. It was not like how rocks might shift slightly beneath the sea; not like that at all. A slow grin spreading over my face, I kicked a stone on purpose and sent it tumbling a dozen paces away. Despite a slight pain in my foot, I chortled in delight, then raced forward to kick another. This one I managed to heave airborne and it soared, at once flying and bound to fall faster than aught within the sea would ever plummet. When I turned to Cora, beaming, she raised a brow.

"Aye, showed that one its place, you did." By which I took her to mean rocks were not allowed along the dirt path, and I ought to kick any we came across. I resolved this was the least way I could repay her hospitality.

At last, sometime before noon, we came to the place she called the chief's ráth, Dùn Beinn. It seemed an earthen mound shaped into wall-like structures, with the defences further reinforced by wooden stakes. I must have stood gawping at it—for though it had none of the grandeur of the sunken ruins I had oft explored, it had vibrant life the likes of which I had never seen—as Cora took my hand and guided me onward. We passed pens of animals making strange, oft pathetic cries, their homes reeking of filth, and I wondered for what purpose the humans had corralled these hairy beasts. We saw people dragging overburdened carts across a bridge that spanned a ditch encircling the ráth. I ogled their goods, for they had vegetables and fruits I had never seen, bright fabrics and circular wooden containers that seemed to slosh with unknown liquids, and more and more. So many new wonders to explore that I could scarce restrain the urge to grab things off any given cart.

When the carters had cleared, Cora led us along the same path and our footfalls clomped along the wooden bridge, making satisfying, hollow sounds. I chuckled for joy at the novelty of such a thing. Curious, I jumped, then revelled in the thump as my feet landed upon the surface. Whilst I could, as a merrow, throw myself from the sea and then splash back down, as dolphins at play were wont to do, it was a rare thing for me. The feeling of the air tugging upon me, pulling back toward the land held a wonderful strangeness, and so I took to jumping every other pace along the bridge.

"Good solid oak, this is," Cora mumbled, "and kind of you to be testing it for them, I suppose."

I had not known bridges needed testing. This was then another service I could provide to Men and thus earn my place among them. Thus, grinning and hopping, I continued forward. The structure ended in giant wooden doors which had been thrown wide, letting a stream of

Men pass in both directions. Someone rode past us on a horse and I could not stop myself from reaching out to stroke the beast.

Cora snatched my wrist and held it tight, eyes wide. "Touch a knight's horse like that, and you may well lose a hand for your trouble."

I recall standing there, all mirth ripped from me in an instant, stupefied at the thought that anyone might maim a person for simply admiring an animal. I remember thinking that the honest savagery of the merrows was surely better than such possessiveness or the malice that seemed to accompany the idea of having something which others did not. Would this knight have imagined I might damage his horse by touching its flank? Did he think its arse so fragile it might break loose with but a nudge?

We crossed into the town and I was overcome fresh stimuli, my disquiet over the horse soon slipping from my mind. There were numerous small huts, all topped with the same grassy stuff as Cora's house had been, though these dwellings looked scarce large enough for a family to all sit down in. I thought it seemed almost a punishment, these people having to live atop one another like molluscs. Or perhaps the ráth was more akin to a reef, and each little home a polyp in which fish might dart about. Once I began to consider the town as a whole to be more of a cohesive entity, I found I could stomach the thought of such close confines. Still, surely such security as came from this place came at the cost of freedom.

There were other buildings, some without walls, where odd animals dwelt. I saw fenced areas where short, pinkish creatures snuffled about in the mud. In another penned section, I saw a pair of creatures I took to be small, hairy horses, though they had curling horns on either side of their heads and made ugly bleating noises. The animal homes smelt even worse than the Man spaces, and I pitied the creatures, contained as they were, denied the freedom to roam where they willed.

As we moved toward the centre of town, the buildings grew finer and I judged them to be houses for the more important families. No longer tiny huts, but rather homes larger than Cora's, where many humans could dwell at once. Unlike the houses on the outskirts, some of these had walls of stones stacked together, as if in crude imitation of the sunken city I had oft visited.

At the heart of the ráth stood the greatest house in Dùn Beinn, many times the size of any of the others, like unto a palace in comparison. Before the structure lounged a pair of men with spears, and Cora spoke to one of them, indicating me with a shift of her head.

"Aye," I heard one say. "Only, Chief's away and won't be back for days yet. Take the foundling to his son and maybe he'll figure on what to do with her." With that, he waved us on.

So it seemed I was to meet the chief's son now.

WHEN I CAME within the great house, my faltering steps had little to do with the stinging in my feet. Cast in bands of light and shadow by sunlight through the high windows, there before me stood Donall, in the midst of what seemed a heated debate. Around him hovered a pair of other men, and though they spoke in guarded tones I could not catch, their postures and gestures bespoke simmering violence.

The house was supported by great wooden columns, carved with spiralling whorls whose import I could not guess. Other shafts of wood crossed overhead, apparently helping keep up the dried-grass roof. There were flat spaces up there, as if people—could they fly—might have deigned to sleep high above their fellows. In the centre of the hall ran a long pit lined with the embers of a dying fire I at once had the urge to try touching. At the fringes, in bowls standing upon iron legs, burnt other fires. The combined effect of so many flames lent the space a hazy quality, stinging my eyes, obscuring my vision. The air smelt odd, thick with smoke and unfamiliar smells. People milled about, some well-dressed, others in plain garb like me and Cora wore. Those in bright, fringe-decorated clothes tended to stand or lounge, served food or drink by the plain-clad folk. Strands of fabric decorated in strange patterns dangled from the roof planks or adorned the walls, spreading life and colour to a place that might have otherwise felt drab. Instead, it felt riotous with sensation, overwhelming, and I could not decide whither to let my gaze linger.

All this I took in, whilst stupefied at finding the man I sought. The Kelpie must have deliberately cast me ashore close to where Donall dwelt, for Inis Fáil was too vast to imagine this coincidence. The waves could have hurled me anywhere here, or even beyond, somewhere on the continent. But the Kelpie had left me within a few hours walk of Donall. It meant the spirit thought to give me a fair chance. Though the entity had claimed my tongue, had gained from me a promise of my very soul should I fail, it seemed to want to make of this a real game. It was one I intended to win, even if I still had scant idea how to claim the heart of a human man. Had I my tongue, I could have used the Voice and had every male in the hall ready to throw themselves at my feet for even a hint of my favour. Was that the reason the Kelpie had taken it from me? Such thoughts made the loss feel all the more bitter, my mouth aching though the wound had healed.

Donall cast a glimpse my way, but no flicker of recognition creased his visage, even when our eyes met, and he turned back toward the men with which he squabbled. I watched him, this chief's son, to whom I had tied my fate. He had a shock of wavy brown hair, thick as a field of seaweed. His eyes were the colour of the midnight sea, and, to me in that moment, seemed just as deep. He was all hard muscles and towering height, and I thought, surely, here was a man accustomed to battle and hardship. I recalled the feel of his flesh against mine, longed to touch it once more.

By my side, Cora squeezed my hand. I cast about to see if she intended to alert me to some peril—ready to bite anyone intending harm—but she was smiling at me, a matronly look of reassurance on her face. Perhaps she sensed the spark of my excitement and mistook it for fear about what place I would find within the ráth, and her concern touched me. I smiled back and returned the light squeeze.

When I looked back, I noticed Donall was again casting surreptitious glances my way. My heart leapt. Could it be he did remember me? Whilst he could be forgiven for not knowing what he'd seen at the time I'd saved him, he had looked on my face. Our gazes met; my pulse leapt. Maybe ... maybe I did not need the Voice. Maybe, if I could win his affections without such a thing, it would have meant far more.

The men Donall argued with broke away, storming out past Cora and me, though one paused at the door to cast a withering glance at Donall. I did not know what went on betwixt these people, but I knew it meant trouble. Resentment festered here, and I thought it unlikely that those I had seen leaving would let it go.

"Who is this?" Donall asked, approaching us as the men ducked out of the hall. His eyes swept over me before settling on my face and lingering there. I could also see him struggling to recall where he had seen me before, and *oh*, how I longed to tell him. I wanted to shout that I had saved his life, that I had risked so very much for him. Part of me wondered if knowing what I had done for him would lead to love. But then, what did I know of such things, really? Too, an urge rose in me, to reach out and cup his cheek with my palm, and barely did I forestall that longing, thinking he might recoil from a woman he had never met.

"A foundling," Cora said with a bow of her head that was, I assumed, a gesture of respect. One I mimicked. "Washed up on the shore. Can't tell us where she's from nor who her people are, poor lass. Can't speak a word on account of ... Well, I thought to bring her to your father and see if he couldn't find a place for her. Me, I couldn't manage such a thing, not in the winter."

"Of course," Donall said with a grave nod. A slight pause. "You ... you're Blair's widow, yeah?"

"Aye, that I am."

Donall nodded, then motioned to some other girl who came scampering over. "Get her a meal and a mug of corma and send her on her way with a couple of bronze coins." Cora dropped into a deeper bow at that, mumbling obsequious thanks. I had gathered Donall was the son of the chief who ruled here, which seemed to make him some sort of prince. "Maybe it'll help with supplies for the winter," he said to Cora, then looked to me. "I suppose you can't well tell me your name, can you?"

I shrugged and shook my head. Until that moment, it had not occurred to me that he would never learn my name, and the thought filled me with sadness. My guts ached with that sorrow. I thought, for a moment, I might burst from the volcanic welling of frustration in my core. He would not know my name. This man, to whom the Kelpie had bound my destiny, would never even speak my name! What bitter twist of Fate permitted such cruel ironies?

Cora bid me farewell and went off with the girl Donall had summoned for her. The chief's son guided me away from my rescuer and out behind the hall, where I stood blinking in the sunlight. Having lived all my life nocturnally, I despaired at the thought of forever having to operate in daylight hours.

"Can you tell me aught of yourself, then?" he asked as he led me between other houses. He was taking me on a tour of the ráth, I realised a moment before he pointed out where various families lived. The place was smaller than Cantref Gwaelod, yet housed even more people, jammed together. Again, I reminded myself these huts were but coral polyps, parts of a whole, nor was it for me to decide how others ought to live. "No," he said after introducing me to a handful of passersby, a blur of names and faces, when his name, his face, were the only ones I cared about at the time. "You can't explain much. Hmm. Have you any skills you can demonstrate?" I frowned at that, uncertain what qualified as skills in a mortal settlement. "Sewing?" he asked. "Weaving, perhaps?" At each, I shook my head, my heart falling. Would he cast me out if he thought me useless, unable to perform any craft? "Candle making? Basket weaving? Can you cook?" He must have seen the expression on my face—for until yesterday I'd never eaten cooked food, much less prepared it—because he chuckled and folded his arms over his chest. I spotted the place where he was missing several fingers on his left hand and, without thinking, I reached for it, sorrowful I had needed to maim him.

A dour look fell over him but he let me take his hand to examine the wound. "Aye," he said. "Well, wasn't as though I was in line to be High King, so the mark against my beauty shouldn't cost me too much. Makes some things more difficult though." The hint of a mischievous smile replaced his fallen look. "Harder dealing with my breeches and such." I did not know what breeches were, but he seemed to expect me to laugh, so I smiled. "Ah, my foundling," he said with a sigh. Despite his bulk, there lurked in his gaze a surprising gentleness, soft as a dolphin's silky skin. "What am I to do with you? No skills to take care of yourself and not a tongue to speak for yourself. Well, I'll not have you out there on your own. Maybe in time you'll learn some trade or other. For now, I suppose you can shadow me. I find myself somewhat bereft of friends of late, and perhaps having someone to talk to would not be amiss." Abruptly, his face fell. "Oh, Epona, what am I saying! I ... forgive me, I did not think." I had no knowledge of who or what Epona was, nor much of his meaning.

Understanding he felt shamed at thinking he had offended, I fiercely waved it away and motioned for him to continue. Perhaps I could not *talk* to him, but I could listen. If that was the one skill I had to offer in this strange place, then I resolved to be the absolute master of that skill. A moment, I lingered, wondering how he might react if I held his hand. Would it prove too hasty? Well, I had not come on land to live timid as a hermit crab. As Cora had taken mine, I took his hand, which for some reason caused the man to raise a brow. Only for a heartbeat though, then he chuckled and resumed walking through town with me.

"You are an odd one, foundling, but perhaps that's just what I needed." He guided me toward a building that, though mostly of wood, had stone blocks in its lower half. "Our metalsmith, Rory, works his craft here. Sometimes into the night, in fact. Well into the night if he gets something up his arse about it. Once he—"

I jerked to a stop aghast at such a thought, hands to my mouth. Yanking my hand from his had spun Donall around and he looked at me a moment in concern before chuckles took him. "Damn. Uh, I didn't mean he literally has aught up his ... that's just an expression, is all, lass. Means he gets obsessed with stuff."

I frowned, considering the strange expression. Did that I mean I had spent most of my life with humans up my arse? I did not think I cared for this turn of phrase much, and I suppose my face showed it, for Donall burst into snickers he seemed to be trying to suppress. Trying and failing.

"Aye, well, anyway." He started to walk away but I lingered, overwhelmed with curiosity about the place where a Man could work smithcraft. Such was a place of legend to us, and it seemed unbelievable to imagine I stood now mere feet away from a forbidden wonder. And too, there was the sort of horror one gets when one knows lethal predators lurk unseen in nearby waters. This place would have worked *iron*, and its mere touch could have burned my skin and stolen my vitality. Were I wise, I would have run from here in an instant. But ...

"Would you care to see his smithy?" Donall asked, following my gaze. "I don't hear the clamour at the moment, which means he's mostlike stopped for a bite. Or more likely a mug of corma. He won't mind if we steal a peek."

I had begun hopping in place at such an offer, grinning. With a chuckle, Donall once more took me by the hand and led me into the darkened space. A low fire simmered within a stone structure that I peered at, careful not to touch any of the numerous iron implements scattered about the room. "That's the furnace," Donall said, then proceeded to point out a few other strange names. Bellows and anvil, tongs and quenching trough. "In truth," he admitted, "I know very little of the art, for it is a secret craft, known to but few. According to the bards, long ago, Gofannon taught his apprentices the lore of bronze and of iron and the hidden knowledge of their working. But the smiths are almost as reticent as druids when it comes to their craft, and it is not for the likes of you or me."

"As if you'd have the wit to ken my meaning," a gruff voice said from behind us. The man who swaggered in was thick as a tree, with arms of corded muscle and a bulging neck. Shirtless, his torso revealed numerous scars and burns, perhaps an effect of his trade, for I took him to be Rory the Smith. I also took Donall's estimation he would not mind our presence to be somewhat mistaken. "You showed your sense well enough already," Rory almost spat at the chief's son. "And now, unless your father can clean this mess of shite you've flung about, I'll be back to making blades and spears instead of nails and tools, I will."

Being all but a prince, I expected Donall to respond in kind to such vitriol, for surely he must have had pride. But instead the chief's son hung his head. "Aye, well, best we be getting back, anyway," he mumbled and all but dragged me from the smithy.

Outside though, I pulled him to a stop and spread my hands in question. My inability to speak felt akin to barnacles abrading my skin, a ceaseless vexation I doubted I would ever become inured against.

Donall frowned, his brows drawn so tight I feared I might have angered him. I could not afford to risk him driving me from his side. If I earned his ire, I had no way to soothe it without words. He heaved a sigh, though. "I think I need a drink afore I'm ready to talk on all that. Wine?"

I shrugged, though I had no idea what sort of drink that might prove.

❧

THE CRIMSON LIQUID he gave me burned going down, and I almost spit it out. At least the first sip. Only my desire to please him and keep him talking kept me drinking. By the time I'd drained the goblet, I found I did not mind the drink so much as I had expected. By the time I was into my second cup, I realised this was an intoxicant, for it left me woozy and lethargic. Certain types of undersea fungi could produce similar effects, though I had not before tried one myself.

Now, I lay sprawled over a deliciously soft fur rug beside the fire pit in Donall's private room, luxuriating in the warmth of the flame. I longed to yank off the itchy dress Cora had given me and let the fire's heat wash over my bare skin, but I feared Donall might think such a thing rude on a first meeting. His chambers were smaller than my grotto, but in his company, I found them cosy rather than cramped. He had a window, now closed off with wooden boards I rather wished he removed to let in the starlight. Piled in one corner, he had numerous hairy animal skins, a place I assumed he used for sleeping. He had kept his wine container sitting on a table low enough he could reach it even whilst reclining.

"Another?" Donall asked, and I shrugged in the happy insouciance this wine seemed to spawn in me. He poured me a third cup and then one for himself. The first he'd drained in a single long swig, and I had tried to imitate him, before gagging on it. "Well, then." He took another sip, then set the mostly full goblet aside. "Suppose I promised you a tale. Hmm." He looked about his chamber as if seeking answers from the leaping shadows the fire sent crawling up his walls. Like the outer hall, his walls bore fabric hangings with patterns somehow meshed into the creation. One, I thought, perhaps showed Men paying homage to a horse. "After the destruction of Kêr-Ys, some, uh ... eighteen years back, there were these rumours. They said one of Gralon's daughters survived, that she somehow wasn't in the city when the waves claimed it, was taken from it as a babe. There are stories that, since the fall, some of the last Knights of Ys have been searching for the lost princess. You've heard the tales, aye?" He looked at me. "No?"

I could only shrug, for I knew so little of human lands or politics. Yet something captivated me in the tale of lost kingdoms and missing princesses. His gaze lingered on my eyes a hair longer than it had prior; had he already begun to fall for me, I wondered? Could this prove so easy to claim his heart?

"Well, I grew up hearing such things. Me and everyone else. Meantime, of course, the whole of Nemedia's gone to shite. I mean, is Inis Fáil even really part of the same kingdom anymore? Too many kings this land has, and each one trying to climb the backs of the others to be the next High King. So most of my life we've had these wars and raids and this bickering, and it never ends. Then one day, this druid, he mentions that if the princess were alive, she'd be the last of the High blood, Nemed's own heir.

"All the clan chiefs, the petty kings, realise what that means. She was a babe then, aye, but now she'd have reached the age of choice and could take a husband. Any man who married her would have a better claim at being High King, maybe the best claim. So some of the other chiefs' sons and I thought we'd be the ones to find her. Thought maybe she'd even choose one of us to wed. Either way, we'd all be heroes, and if there was a High King, maybe we'd have peace again. A foul jest, that."

For a time, he lost himself in his wine, and I sipped at mine, revelling in the novelty of the experience. It engendered an odd warmth in my belly I found soothing, even if the experience of constantly falling—despite lying down—was a little unnerving. Besides, I liked the sound of his voice and the timbre of his story. I imagined him speaking thus for hour upon hour, me but looking into the midnight blue of his eyes.

"We took a ship and started a hunt for clues, seeking the lass. Madness, maybe, since she was taken ere she had a name, and we'd no idea what she looked like, save flaxen-haired. But, you know, the thought of glory can get a man drunker than any wine." He cast aside his empty goblet as if to emphasise that point. "One day, we spied this magnificent horse on the strand, and something overcame us. We *had* to claim the beast. That thought drowned out all others, even our desire to find the lost princess. We all knew the tale of the Kelpie, how it could take forms like those of Man or horse and drown its victims. We knew but thought it fancy. Who among us had ever laid eyes on a Sluagh or other fae, much less stranger beings?

"So mount we did, and then the Kelpie ran into the sea to drown us. We … couldn't let go. Our hands held fast to the creature, though I cannot explain the how of it. After that, I don't know. There was a blur and I was drowning, and something … someone … shite." He held up his left hand for me to examine his missing fingers. "My hand was torn free, whilst all my fellows were dragged down to the Otherworld." He sucked a sharp breath down at that. "When I had recovered enough to journey, I had to come home and tell my father what had happened. And he had to tell the fathers of the others they had lost their sons. So I'm alive and they're all dead, and it means everyone holds me to account for the mistakes we all made, and I can't say as I blame them for that. Even my own people know I'll have brought war down on them. Sooner or later, the chiefs and kings will come for blood over what they've lost. Ah ... so, my foundling. I fear your benefactor shan't prove the finest friend you could have found."

I shook my head in denial, though the motion was languid and I mostly just rolled over in front of the fire. I would show him he was wrong, I resolved. I would show him ...

I RODE LIKE THE WIND, skirting the coast, racing down the trail. Not just the wind, the whirlwind, sweeping down with promise. My hair streamed behind me, billowing free, my cloak tugging at my neck as it flew.

My heart raced, eagerness so sharp I could taste it upon my tongue. There is joy in speed, in the pounding of pulses, in the rush of life. Whatever one's purpose, there is vibrance in life.

There is wrath when it is stolen. There is grief.

No, no grief could show upon my face, as I drew nigh to the city along the shore. Open gates and open arms awaited me, an embrace. I did not want to dwell on that either. A means to an end.

There would be feasting and music, laughter and dancing. The press of bodies, the rush of wine. The closeness that would follow, in private rooms.

Forward, forward, Morvoren panting, sweat glistening on the mare as well. I slowed, could not seem too eager.

But the city rose before me, larger than most, smaller than one.

The sun was shining, warm on my face, as I slowed my mount to a trot and rode through those gates. Beyond, I would find a rich castle, a rich king drunk on his glory. Hungry for life, hungry for me, so the phial at my side assured me.

Riding through the bustling market, I imagined the look upon his wife's face as he cast her aside. Her shame, wrath. It was due; I had no pity for her. Relished, even, the thought of anguish stirred here, in this place.

Before the castle, in the city of Bro Érech, I dismounted. Walked Morvoren to the stables and saw her tended to.

When no one watched, I downed the contents of the phial at my side.

Such plans I had for my evening. Such grand designs.

I AWAKENED to morning's harsh assault, filtering in through the overhead windows.

After hearing Donall's story, the ripple of memory that had haunted my dreams became a tsunami. I knew now, without a doubt, that in my past life I had been the princess Dahut. Though I could not recall the whole of her life, of *my* life, the torrent of fractured memories was enough it could wash me away if I let it. I wondered, if I pushed hard enough down this channel, if I would risk becoming more Dahut than Lí Ban. I wondered if that would be so wrong.

They said one of Gralon's daughters survived, that she somehow wasn't in the city when the waves claimed it, was taken from it as a babe. His words played through my mind, danced with momentous import.

My head throbbed with the wine and the revelation that had come over me, and for a long time, I lay on Donall's floor, listening to the comforting sound of his snores. I felt anew the grief of the loss of my baby sister, though I had never known her in this life. It was as if, whatever scabs time and my own death had allowed to grow over that wound, now they had been torn away, and my soul bled once more. I felt the guilt, for I knew her abduction had been *my* fault, and it was a burden I could not bear. It pressed upon me like a physical weight until each breath I must take became a fresh battle, and no matter how many times I won, still the war of it would not end.

I saw, in my mind's eye, the crashing waves that drowned the city of Kêr-Ys, and me along with it. So much death, the greatest jewel of Man washed from the Earth. Naught could bring back the glory of that fallen city, I knew, and naught could make up for the mistakes I had made.

But ... if the tales Donall believed were true, my sister yet lived. Why could I not remember what had happened to the babe? Every which way I tossed the memories about in my mind, I saw only flickers, images rising up from the currents of a maelstrom, visible for a moment before they were sucked below the surface once more. I knew, back then, as Dahut, I dedicated my life to finding the girl. I would have done aught then to find her. I would do even more now.

Donall believed my sister could save the crumbling kingdom of Nemedia. Certainly I saw peace as a worthy goal, but the truth was, I needed to find my sister for her sake and for mine. I could never know peace so long as these memories so haunted my dreams, seeping even into my waking hours. If I could help save her kingdom in the process, that would prove a welcome boon.

The sparking of my hope sieved off my grogginess and filled me with an energy as powerful as any amount of anáil. I scrambled to my feet, heedless of how they hurt, and took to pacing about Donall's chambers. How was I to begin to explain to him what I needed? I could not tell my tale nor in any way share what I knew. Some humans, I had heard, recorded knowledge by scratching markings on wood or stone, but I knew of no such art.

In taking my tongue from me, the Kelpie had taken all I relied upon or ever known. With a frustrated huff, I ran my fingers through my hair, only to find them snagging in tangles. When had I last attended to my locks? Tending to one's hair was a daily ritual in Cantref Gwaelod, but since gaining legs, I had scarcely thought of such things. I do not recall much about my mother, but I remember when she died. I was very young, and I recall lying on the floor of my father's grotto, yelping like a wounded seal. My grandmother came to me—I think Father sent her, not knowing how to handle a grieving child nor perhaps how to bear his own grief—and she settled beside me and took to fixing my wild black hair. "We must always look our best, child," she said, "for others will take their cues on how to treat us based on the way we carry ourselves." She had a dozen oysters attached to her tail then, and she clamped a pair on mine as well. I yelped, the pain in my body a momentary distraction from that of my heart. "Beauty is pain, Lí Ban," she said. "Maybe so is love."

The memory reminded me I was supposed to be winning Donall's heart. I knew, of course, that such a mission was more pressing than finding a sister missing for almost two decades. Should he bind himself to another, I would be lost and then I could not help my sister anyway. Too, I recalled Donall's words. *Any man who married her would have a better claim at being High King, maybe the best claim.* But I *was* Dahut, reborn. If I could tell him thus, perhaps he'd want to marry me. Once, I thought the idea of making a lifelong oath to bind myself to another a foul constraint. Now, besides proving needful because of my bargain with the Kelpie, I found such a fancy ... not unpleasant at all. Still, stirred by my dreams, the loss of the baby girl felt unbearably urgent. Was that Dahut's need or my own? Did such a question even matter?

Taking Grandmother's words to heed, I set to fixing my hair and thinking on how I could investigate so old a disappearance, and without speaking. In the end, my tangles were gone long before my problem.

With a groan, Donall awakened. When he looked on me, his eyes widened. "Oh, gods. The whole palace will think we ..."

It took me a moment to apprehend his meaning. He meant they must have assumed that having stayed in the same room, we were now mated. I did not see why this should prove a problem—indeed, it *might* have helped me create the love I needed from him—but the idea appeared to vex him. Perhaps the laws of Man prevented so ranking a person from choosing a mate of unknown blood? I must have screwed up my face, wondering how else I might win his affections if not by words or the allure of my body, for his expression grew graver still.

"Don't worry. These things pass in time, my foundling, and none will think ill of you."

Of me? What strange notions was he on about now? Well, such things could not concern me at the moment. Not with the pressing need to find my sister.

INTERLUDE: DAHUT

With the knowledge gained from Elouan's trance, the knights of Ys scoured the countryside for Black Annis and the stolen babe. Dahut, however, had never been one to sit and wait for others to attend to her troubles. Some princesses could idle in their bowers and await word from afar.

Not Dahut.

She travelled between village and ráth, consulting druids and wise women. She took counsel from knights sworn to petty kings and the fianna of Inis Fáil. Ever she quested for the Sluagh who had stolen from her that which she could not bear to lose.

In another nemeton, this one uphill from the rushing water of the Danu, nigh upon the border of Starfall Vale, she chanced upon the chief druid Donn. Dahut had tied her mare to a hickory tree outside the oak grove. The first shock of autumn chill had turned the leaves the colour of flames, sun dappled by the afternoon glare. The pleasant weather would not last, though. The wind spoke of a coming storm. It was not visible on the horizon yet, but Dahut's training included weather witchery, and she always knew before the rains came, or the snows, or the miasma-like fog that sometimes swept over her lowland home.

Fallen leaves crunched under her boots as she trod into the grove. Donn sat upon a rock, watching her approach. The chief druid had a timelessness to him and he'd held the position long, she knew. Even in the days of her mother, he'd been chief druid, and still, he had a thick head of dark hair and a full beard. Perhaps he knew some other arcana that had slowed his aging, but if so, he kept that knowledge for himself alone.

"'Tis not enough," Dahut said without preamble. "I hunt across the land and still, the months drag on. Still, I find no hair of her." And little more of the monster that took her. "I must do more."

"What do you ask of me?"

Dahut hesitated. When she'd seen him here, a plan had come to her, wild, untrammelled by reason. Such were the passions of the desperate, running swifter even than the currents of the Danu. "Aodh once told me of my mother. How she had been but a miller's daughter until she met a wizard." The chief druid frowned. "You know of it, too. Tell me and tell me true, Donn. If this man can help me now—"

"You speak as though this wizard were some patron to your line, but I assure you, naught could prove further from the case."

Dahut settled down before him and clutched his hand. "Tell me, I beseech you. If there is the faintest chance ..."

Donn sighed, his shoulders sagging. "Aye, she was the daughter of a miller, living on the edge of the Black Forest. Her father, wanting to seem high before the knights, once bragged his daughter had such talent at the spinning wheel, she could spin straw into gold. A father's pride in his child, and words that ought not have been spoken.

"Word of it came to your grandfather, Kenan, and he had the girl Dieub locked in a tower in his palace. He bade her do as her father had claimed, or else the man would be whipped as a liar. Of course, Dieub could do no such thing, and alone at night, in that tower, she wept. Then came the wizard, who agreed to perform the task if she would grant him a boon.

"Your mother's family had lost much, but once, in the days when Owain ap Nemed ruled their lands, they had been knights. And Dieub had an heirloom of those days, a necklace of engraved pearl, said to have been crafted by the sirens of Pontus, in the Inner Sea. This, she gave to the wizard, and he did as he had claimed and spun all the straw into fine, golden thread.

"The sight of such wonders inflamed Kenan's greed, and the next night, he brought an even larger pile of straw and bade her spin that, as well. Dieub knew, were she to refuse, she and her poor father would now be doomed, for the king would think her not unable, but unwilling to obey. Once more the wizard appeared in the dark of night, but this time, Dieub had naught to offer him. Naught, save herself, and thus she agreed to lie with him if he would spin more straw into gold.

"Morning came and the king saw a yet greater coil of woven gold thread. Kenan was a cunning man, and as such, perhaps we might account him a good king. For he knew, should he let anyone else claim a girl with such power as this, the wealth could prove a threat to the royal line of Kêr-Ys. Therefore, he proclaimed, if Dieub could spin an entire room full of straw into gold, she would be wed to his son, the Prince Gralon, your father.

"Your mother wished to refuse, for though marrying the prince would restore all her family had lost and then some, she had no means to perform such a feat. Yet she held silent. She knew, no excuse she could make now would satisfy the king. So when the wizard came again, she beseeched him to work his wonder one last time. But he had already taken her treasure and enjoyed the pleasures of her flesh, and she had no idea what to offer him.

"The wizard, however, knew what he sought. 'You will give me your firstborn.' I do not know what went through your mother's heart then. Perhaps she considered it was better to die and let her father die than sacrifice a child thus. Perhaps she thought it better those living should remain so, even if it meant she would lose a babe that did not yet exist. Either way, she agreed. And then the wizard tapped a finger to her abdomen and winked, for he knew already her womb had quickened with his child.

"He spun the straw once more and filled the room with gold. And your father and your mother were wed."

As the telling had drawn on, Dahut's fingers had dug furrows in the dirt. "I ... I was promised to this wizard." And it would mean Gralon was not her father.

"No, Dahut," Donn said, his smile full of sorrow. "Not you."

"But I am the firstborn, I am the heir of Ys."

"You are the heir, but not the firstborn. Your mother repented her decision as the babe grew within her, and trusted the truth to your

father, for his wisdom and kindness won her. Gralon allowed everyone
to believe the babe his. The child came, a girl. Then, in the night, came
the wizard.

"Neither the prince nor his wife wished to honour the bargain, but
they realised breaking a pact with a wizard might cost them greatly. So
they begged, and at last the man relented and made them a new bargain:
if, within three nights, they could guess his name, they could keep the
child. If not, he would take the princess, and he would plunder the
prince's treasures. Desperate, they agreed.

"They made many guesses as to his name, but none held true. So
they sent knights riding the land, hunting for word of the wizard. On the
last day, the last of those knights learnt of the King of the Golden Mountain, a wizard—or perhaps an *Other*—who ruled there, by the name of
Rumpelstiltskin.

"And when the wizard came to them, the queen proclaimed his
name. And the wizard grinned an evil grin and looked from Prince
Gralon to your mother and to the babe. 'That's a name, but it is not my
true name.' And so the wizard took the newborn princess and left her
parents to grieve." Donn paused, and he squeezed her hand. "A little over
a year later, you were born, the new heir to Kêr-Ys, the princess Dahut."

Dahut could hardly draw breath. She had *another* stolen sister, one
taken by this wizard, but surrendered willingly by her parents. "I ..."

"You wonder, perhaps, what other treasure this Rumpelstiltskin
claimed from the prince? None can say for certain, but I have my
guesses. For the next morn, King Kenan was found, dead in his sleep,
face locked in a grimace and flesh turned sallow." Another pause. "So,
this, Dahut, is the truth of the wizard you ask over, who I think may not
even be a Man. And if Aodh told you of him, it was as a warning, not
something for you to chance on and grasp for in your own moment of
desperation. Do not ignore the lesson of your mother."

"My mother ..." Dahut pulled free her hand and stood, stiff. "Are you
certain you learnt the right lesson from the tale? Had my mother not
trusted the wizard, she would be dead, and neither I nor any of my
sisters would live."

"Dahut ..."

"I will find my sister!" she shrieked. All else could be dealt with in the
fullness of time. But for the babe, she could not wait.

THE GOLDEN MOUNTAIN lay on the edge of the Enchanted Forest, itself a stretch of forbidden woodland across the river Albia, the northernmost boundary of Nemedia. Once, Dahut would never have dared to cross outside the Kingdoms of Man. The Kingdoms had dangers aplenty, and only the reckless or well armed ventured far past home. But beyond, the wilds loomed vast and unknowable, an ever-encroaching circle around the lands held by Man.

No bridges spanned the Albia and, though the waters were not so very wide, no ferries ventured crossings. The river marked the threshold of where any dare tread and, so far as the peoples of northern Nemedia were concerned, the far side might as well have been the Otherworld itself. Dahut stood upon the bank, watching the current stream by, her foot on the rim of a rowboat. Fishermen did plumb the lake just upstream of here—from them she had bought the boat—though it lay perilously close to the Hinterlands of Falias.

As, indeed, did the Golden Mountain itself, nestled among the Crownpeaks that formed the northern crest of the world. Savages lurked in the tundras beyond those mountains, brutal people best left apart from the rest of Mankind.

Dahut wished she'd been able to find Sétanta or Moccus. She wished one of her knights could have accompanied her on this mad voyage. For the first time in her life, true terror gripped her heart, and she dreaded the thought of crossing these waters alone.

"I am the whirlwind, Aveldro," she whispered. "I am the whirlwind." Heart hammering, she shoved the boat into the ice-blue waters and hopped in. She repeated the refrain again and again as she tugged at the oars, heaving herself into the unknown.

Before long, her arms burnt with the strain of fighting the current, which sought to carry her away from the mountain, toward the North Sea. "I am the whirlwind!" she rasped, through gritted teeth. Her muscles roared in protest. "I. Am. Aveldro!"

By the time she reached the far bank, her palms were raw, the skin chapped and peeling. Shaky, Dahut stumbled from the boat and collapsed upon the bank. Slowly, she lifted her gaze to the tree line. Though the wood was dense, it was no darker than the edge of the Black

Forest, south of Nemedia. Indeed, here, she saw more flowers. Creeping vines bursting with dianthus and peonies, though she thought the flowers wrong for such. She could not shake the impression the vines moved, yet never could she see it happen, no matter how hard she stared.

Somewhere, from deep inside the wood, a wolf howled. Legend claimed this wood was the final resting place of Edern the Eternal, that it served as a mighty cairn for the demigod. If so, the Enchanted Forest ensured none would ever pay homage to the fallen child of Nemed.

Dahut pushed herself up and brushed the sand from her palms and riding breeches, then tightened her cloak around her shoulders. If she skirted the woods, she could reach the foothills, and from there to the Golden Mountain. A blanket of fog had rolled in, masking details, but she could make out the peak in the far distance. A tributary of the Albia, one spilling down from the Crownpeaks, still separated her from the Hinterlands of Falias, a land even more twisted than the Enchanted Forest, into which she dare not venture.

Though she had set out from the village in the morn, it had taken her longer than she'd hoped to make the crossing, and she began to doubt she'd reach the mountain ere eventide. The last thing she could afford was to be caught out, alone at night, on the threshold of the Hinterlands. If that happened, she might be better off taking her chances in the Enchanted Forest rather than risk being spotted by the Wild Hunt.

Not far beyond the river, the land began to slope steeply upward, and Dahut missed Morvoren all the more. She'd had to leave the mare back at the village, had no way to get her across the Albia, and anyway, the animal might have panicked once she reached the Golden Mountain. Once she laid eyes upon ... whatever was beyond. Animals, they had senses Men lacked and tended to grow skittish when the world thinned and the Otherworld drew nigh. So Dahut traipsed on, on foot, at the swiftest pace she thought she could maintain, her breaths deep.

It did not take long before chill sweat trickled down the back of her neck. She wished she'd had a few sips of wine to steady her nerves. No, but confronting the wizard aught save stone sober would have been a mistake. Their ilk—and she had not forgotten Donn's supposition Rumpelstiltskin could be an Other—they trafficked in mystery, in obfuscation, in trickery. A lot of so-called magic came from knowing things others didn't and playing that up. The secret lore of plants and animals, of herbs or metals, these things made one seem possessed of supernatural cunning, and druids knew it all too well. It wasn't to say that things beyond the World of Men didn't exist.

Black Annis had proved that, too, as if a druid could have a doubt. Spirits and Others were real, watchful, lurking just out of sight, yet ever plying their subtle influences.

So, sober it was, even as Dahut's frayed nerves roared in anxious protest, her palms clammy, her breath—frosting the air now as she ascended higher—shaky.

A burbling brook cut across her path, shallow enough, though the waters this time of year would be frigid. If she removed her boots, she risked her toes taking frostbite. If damp soaked through her boots, she'd be even worse off, with no dry footwear to don once on the other side. She considered for a moment before sitting and tugging off her boots. She'd have to make a fire to warm herself on the far side, which would delay her more, but she saw little real choice in the matter.

In druidic training, once she'd seen a miller come for aid, his feet peeling and rotten from cold water in winter. They had to amputate one, it had turned so foul. Even a delay was better than risking that.

So she rolled her breeches over her knees, eased one foot into the icy water, yelped, and then plunged the other foot. The water rose to her shins, and she stood, shivering, gasping from the shock of it. No way but forward, even if she felt not the least bit a whirlwind at the moment. Careful of her footing, she trudged across, the waters, at the deepest, splashing her knees and leaving the edges of her breeches sodden.

Then she was across and desperately gathering kindling for a small fire. She ought to have done this before crossing, she thought belatedly. She ought to have planned a great deal of things differently. But how did one *plan* for venturing into unknown perils where none dared tread? The only thing to return from these slopes were whispers and legends and a fear one could not quite put into words.

For a time she sat by the fire, warming her legs and feet—and, aye, her hands, as well—and delaying when she could afford no delay. Trying to tell herself she'd still make it. She had to make it.

With a grunt, she smothered the flames with dirt, then yanked her boots back on. She needed to move, needed to make haste, for she'd lost too much time in this. Beneath the light of day, it was easy to think the banalities of travel—frostbitten toes and chills—the fears most deserving of attention. As the gloaming crept in, though, and the sky began to bruise, a wise woman knew the rising of true dread.

Druids sometimes had to go out at night, it was true, for the sunlight seemed to push the Otherworld farther from the Mortal Realm. If you wished to traffic with Others, with spirits, it was best done under moonlight, under stars, rather than in the harsh glare of day. But, always with care.

Her path now felt wild, artless, as if she were a child bumbling around in the dark, too young to realise her peril. Onward, she pushed, upward, until dustings of snow began to cover the rocks. An early snowfall, perhaps, or maybe it had never melted from the year prior. The hoarfrost grew thicker the higher she climbed, ice catching the gleam of the failing light.

Then she was there.

Upon a plateau on the mountain, rimmed by snow-covered expanses, rose the castle, its towers like desiccated fingers reaching toward the gathering twilight. Sheets of rime crusted over the parapets, obscuring gargoyles, but not quite hiding the dilapidated state of the walls. For in places, the stone had cracked and fallen, worn away by centuries of mountain gales and merciless gnawing of time's jaws. The whole place looked as though it might tumble over. All of it a ruin, save for the twin doors, decorated as they were with gilded trim wrought into intricate whorls. The last light of the setting sun glinted off gold inlays half obscured by layers of ice.

A warning that darkness would soon swallow this place.

Dahut hesitated a moment, only. Then she pushed open one of the doors and trod into the keep.

PART III

Whilst Nemed reigned a god among Men, their kingdom burgeoning in days of glory, word came to him of the plight of his former brethren upon Inis Fáil. For with the retreat of the Firbolg the fomorii rose to dominate the island and oppress the Ellyllon, exacting tribute beyond measure. From their Tower of Glass did they reign, to bring low the Tylwyth Teg, dominating land and sea. This, to Nemed, was a thing not to be borne.

— Annals of Findias, history of the Tylwyth Teg

3

Donall's father, the clan chief, returned a few days later, grim faced and dour. He took long private counsels with his son and a visiting druid who Donall said was named Donn. Donall had given me a room beside his and taken to telling others I was his personal servant. It suited me well enough, and after some instruction, I had learnt how to tidy the room, when to bring his wine, and how to prepare his clothes for the morn or for sleep. These duties, I pursued with verve, eager to please. When he happened to favour me with a smile for a job well attended, my face would flush. I studied, with greater attention than ever I had paid my tutors, his every like and dislike, striving to earn myself one of those smiles.

While Donall took his counsels, I was washing the linens with well water. He had not asked me to do such things, but I felt myself bursting with nervous energy from remaining unable to further my investigation. The other servants were only too happy to show me how to do the chores, once they understood my pantomiming, and I set about beating the laundry with gusto. It was the first occasion I'd had to vent my growing ire since being rendered unable to speak, and I soon realised—from the sound of the wet *thwacks* and the way the maids' eyes widened —my merrow strength remained to me. I was no longer a merrow but nor was I quite of Man. I wondered, then, if my nature was, in fact, closer to our Tylwyth Teg cousins than to humans. Either way, I had to suppress a grin, for much though I had changed, some part of me remained what I had always been. There is a comfort in continuity, I think, in sameness savoured even in a place where all seems alien.

Such were thoughts on my mind when Donall emerged from his meeting, looking as grave as I had ever seen him. He summoned me with but a glance and I fell in step beside him. I wondered if I ought to take his hand, then. We had not touched each other that way since the day he'd taken me on a tour of the ráth, and now an unnameable anxiety rose in me at the thought of his flesh brushing mine. At the fear, should he chance to pull away. In the end, I managed to move but a finger before giving over.

"Can you ride?" he asked me as we came back to his large house. I shook my head, and he frowned. "Well, let's see about getting you a lesson then. I've got a pressing desire to get away from here."

The thought both frightening and intrigued. I had a fascination with horses, true, but I had not the first idea what to do with one if I caught it. Nor could I imagine many animals appreciating people sitting upon them.

We stopped by his chambers where he snatched up a fabric-wrapt bundle and handed it to me. "That dress will impede you on horseback," he said, "so I had the seamstress make a tunic and breeches for you. She took a guess at your size, but I think she got a good length."

A foolish grin burst over my face at the gift and I dropped my dress in a heartbeat.

"Esus's balls!" Donall started, spun to turn his back. "I didn't expect you to just ..."

Uncertain what he was on about, I tugged the breeches up over my legs. They were too snug, clinging to me like another skin I longed to peel off. With the dress, I could at least feel the air upon my legs. I'd seen men, and some few women, dressed in these things, but I had never imagined they would prove so uncomfortable. I was grunting and groaning, tugging at where the fabric rode up on my crotch, when he turned around. Then there was more huffing and turning of his back again. "Could you maybe put the tunic on to cover your ... I mean they're very nice, but ..."

Pulling a face at the confining fabric, I did as Donall asked and yanked the tunic over my head. Then I tapped him on the shoulder and spread my arms to ask his opinion. Crimson seemed to have crept up his neck when he looked again, though it soon faded. With a satisfied nod, he handed me sandals. Once I laced those, he led me outside and to the stables.

From within he drew forth a roan mare whose eyes shone with intellect and, I dared to hope, kindness. "This is Haggis," he told me. Whilst I did not know what the word meant, he said the name with such reverence I assume it must have represented something sacred, something beautiful. A goddess, perhaps? He bade me pet her neck and scratch her ears. A shiver of excitement shot through me at touching the graceful animal, who did not seem to mind the attention in the least.

Donall saddled the animal and swung onto her back, then helped me up behind him. He guided me to wrap my arms around his waist to keep my position. The nearness of him left me feeling flushed, warm not only from the heat seeping off his back but from within myself. I felt the muscles of his abdomen under my palm, experienced a strange thrill at touching them. Did I thrill thus because I knew I needed to win his heart? It was not an onerous task. I pulled myself a hair closer, my pulse pounding.

Donall started us off at a gentle walk; the pace sent my heart aflutter and I laughed. The sound I had made was wheezy and immediately I hated it, my mood turning bitter once again at what I had lost. I knew it did not behove me to dwell on something I would never have back, but I could little help it. Outside the gates, Donall pushed the animal to a faster pace, and the thrill of it chased away my dolours almost at once. Next I knew, I was clinging to him, afraid I'd be thrown. I couldn't imagine the animal could go any faster.

Spurred by my reaction, he proved me wrong by kicking the horse into a run. I wanted to scream but even that sounded more a moan. Donall must have sensed my distress, for he eased off, bringing us back to a walk. He looked back at me, holding my gaze, his eyes assuring me I'd been in no real danger. "You want to get down?" Though I considered it a moment, I shook my head. "Good," he said and rode on.

☙

WE RODE TO THE SEASIDE, which it turned out did not lie so far from the ráth as it first felt. Looking upon the crashing waves, my heart both soared and ached all at once. I felt as though the tide might wash away my soul and thus carry from me all my burdens. I closed my eyes and let the sound of lapping water take me.

It was a momentary thing, though.

"You like the sea?" Donall asked.

I started then, seeing his intense gaze upon me, setting my skin atingle. How long had he watched me thus? What unknowable thoughts danced through his mind when he looked upon me? I wondered if he saw me only as a friend, or as a woman, now, here by the shore. Our gazes held just long enough, I thought, perhaps, perhaps ...

Then his gaze turned, the moment broke like the waves, tumbling away and leaving but a memory, as ever waves must. Did I like the sea, he had asked? Oh, such a question! There are times when the swell of emotions within one grows vast beyond all labels or explanations. I loathed the sea which had forever denied me my dreams until the moment I had torn pieces of myself away to escape it. I longed for it, its song beckoning me as surely as the siren songs of my people called sailors to their dooms. I missed the way the water massaged every part of me, though I had never noticed such a thing until it was gone. I revelled in my freedom to walk and explore the world as it now unfolded before me, even as I mourned for the world I had lost in the process.

Did I like the sea? In it, I saw the manifest evidence for a simple fact: though I might claim whatever I wished for, I could never have *everything* I wanted. Life was like the tides, some part always receding even as what we sought drew within reach. We seized new chances even as memories ached in our souls.

I do not know what Donall read in my expression, but he took my hand and squeezed it, as Cora had done. Perhaps the gesture was meant to express solidarity? Either way, the warmth of his grasp sent a shudder through me, left me hoping he would not let go. I was supposed to win his heart because the Kelpie had thus ordained it, but my eagerness toward that pursuit ran deeper than any bargain. I could feel my pulse beating in my neck, my heart hammering.

"The Corryvreckan is out there, near the mouth of the strait." Donall pointed into the distance, and I nodded, for I well knew where the Kelpie dwelt. "The others, they drowned there." He sucked air between his teeth. Through his hand still wrapt around mine, I felt him trembling. "What fools we were, thinking to be heroes."

Not knowing what else to do, I squeezed his hand back, then withdrew my own—mourning the sudden lack of warmth, the memory of his touch—struck by an inspiration. I knelt in the wet sand and traced the best outline I could manage of the sunken ruins I had so oft visited. I was only imagining what its outline would have looked like prior to its fall, but Donall knelt over me, curious.

"Is that Kêr-Ys?" he asked. I nodded, as pleased with myself as a pufferfish. I had never before attempted to create such a thing, and if he could tell what I meant, I must have made a decent show of it. "Never did I lay eyes upon it," he said. "I was but a small boy when it fell, but Father's described it, and bards' tales conjure images of the great sea walls. They say the Smith Lord, the son of Nemed himself, built the place as a wonder."

I scooted over, giving myself more space to work, then traced the outline of a babe, as best I could. In truth, it was more circles than aught else. I found sketching a person far more challenging than the rough outline of the fallen city.

"I don't ..." he said. This wasn't working, and I needed him to understand me. Changing tactics, I pantomimed suckling a babe at my breast. "Child." Donall spread his hands. "An infant." I pointed at the outline of Kêr-Ys. "A child of Kêr-Ys?" I must have had the most foolish grin imaginable, for he chuckled and beamed at my expression. "A child of ... You mean the lost princess!"

I nodded, absurdly pleased, euphoric, even. He grasped I wanted to discuss her, and there was a thrill in having reached even so small an understanding betwixt us. But how to explain I needed to find her? I had vague memories of her abduction, but I had no way to communicate that. Now I spread my hands and swept my arms over the expanse of land, as if to ask where we could look.

"Assuming she lives at all, I've not the faintest idea where to search. We were fools, me and the others, thinking we could manage such a thing. Lads, drunk on our dreams, is all. Now, my father travelled to the other clans whose sons perished in that damned voyage, trying to soothe things. 'Tis no avail, though. I think I've no choice but to go myself and plead for forgiveness. 'Tis a slim chance, but if I can avert war, I've got to try." He sighed. "Not so keen to leave you behind, though, my foundling."

Leave me behind? My eyes widened at the thought and I lurched up and snatched both his hands, squeezed. He yelped and I released him, realising I was not meant to press with such force.

"Aye, well I'd just as soon take you with me for someone to talk to. But if any of the chiefs take it in their head to avenge their boys on me —"

I once more seized his hand and fervently shook my head. Until this moment, until he spoke of leaving me behind, I had not realised how attached I had become in so short a time. I could not afford to be parted from him. More, I did not *want* to be parted from him, though his favour toward me yet seemed more of friendship than love. Or was it? It was so hard to read such things in him.

Not so keen to leave you behind, though, my foundling. He called me his. He always called me his. Was that endearment only friendship, or somewhat more? Either way, when I thought of the future, I saw only myself by his side, friends or otherwise. I saw us hunting for my lost sister. I saw us spending the quiet evenings as we oft did, my mind lulled toward sleep by the sound of his soothing voice, by rich wines. If he was to ride into danger, I would ride behind him, even as I had done this day. And too, I little minded the closeness such a ride demanded, my chest pressed against his back, warm and strong.

"I could not bear it if you came to harm for my sake," he said after a moment's hesitation. Quirking a smile and freeing my hand from his, I raised fists in front of my face and mimed landing a punch. "Really?" He laughed, running a hand through his windswept hair. "Well, I'd be glad of company anyway. I suppose we ought to claim some supplies and set out in the morn."

LONG WE RODE, and I found my legs and arse ached from the bouncing of the horse. By the time we dismounted, I was walking awkwardly, the skin on my thighs chafed raw. If there is a trick riding these beasts, one did not grow up learning it in Cantref Gwaelod. Still, we passed the time not unpleasantly, for Donall talked of his childhood and his friendship with one of the other chief's sons, Iain, whose father we now called on. Donall had fostered here for a time, he told me, and thus he hoped to find favour with the chief of Sgitheanach. It was a small island off the northern tip of Inis Fáil, and one we could reach in a day if we pushed ourselves, he assured me.

According to Donall, until the fall of Kêr-Ys, an isthmus had connected Inis Fáil to the continent. "No one knows how the great sea wall of the city had failed, but when it did, all Llŷr's fury broke and washed away the isthmus, making Inis Fáil an island in true." From what I had learnt so far, prior to that, it had been a part of Nemedia, both halves ruled by the High King of Kêr-Ys. Small wonder then the lands of Nemedia lay in chaos in the wake of such a cataclysm.

Having lost their king and capital, Men grew weaker, more vulnerable to the predations of the Sluagh. Collectively, the four cities of Tylwyth Teg were named Dark Faerie, at least by Men. The Sluagh were the direst of the four clans, the founders of Falias, the closest of those four cities. Merrows in the Mortal Realm have scant chance—or misfortune—to have dealings with our other fae cousins, and thus I had never seen a Sluagh. Or perhaps, if I had, I could not tell them from humans. From what I could tell, Men saw even less of them and feared them all the more than we did. They dreaded all connected to the Otherworld with a terror beyond mere words, and not without reason. What, then, would Donall make of me, should he ever chance to learn my origins? Would I still be *my foundling*, then? I think my fear of that answer ran deeper even than his dread of the fae, whom they called Others.

All day we had followed the coast, but now we came to the land's edge. A suspended bridge hung precariously over the gap between this island and Sgitheanach, creaking and swaying in the wild breeze. The thing was made of rope with boards somehow attached to make for a crossing. Beneath the span, a fall of dozens of feet that would have us crashing into jagged rocks and thrown into the sea. From here, the current would probably drag our corpses down to the Corryvreckan, for we had seen it in the distance as we followed the coast. If that happened, perhaps even our souls would not escape doom. Thus, I looked on the bridge with about as much trust as I would have afforded a great white shark that hadn't eaten in a fortnight. This bridge, I thought, I would not chance jumping up and down on.

"You wanted to come, foundling," Donall teased. "Let your courage not falter now."

I rolled my eyes, and he led the horse to a stable nearby. Donall greeted the man working within by name, exchanged a few pleasantries, and handed over his mount, before returning to my side. "Just take it slow and follow as I do," he advised as we approached the bridge. I wondered what he would have said had I told him I only learnt to walk a few days back. Not that I had the least way to communicate such a bizarre claim, nor would he have believed me had he understood. With a hand on either side of the rope railing—I felt a fresh pang of guilt that his left hand could scarce grip aught here—he eased onto the bridge. The wood groaned under his weight, making me wince.

But soon he was making his slow progress, and I had no choice save to follow or be left behind. I placed one foot on the first plank. It did not immediately give way and try to pitch me down to the doom below, which I counted a victory. There was something wondrous about being airborne, about being pulled invariably landward, and the sense of flight after leaping. Still, I did not think this the place to enjoy that passion. So I wrapt hands around the ropes and edged forward. I had thought Donall had gone slowly, but the pace I managed would have made a sea slug look swift. Looking back at me, Donall paused partway and let me come to him, then gripped my arm. "Come on, then. It's not so bad as all that."

It must have been more awkward for him, one arm held behind him to hold my hand as I clutched the rope, but we made it across thus. On the far side, I fell to my knees, gasping in relief. Only after Donall had pulled me to my feet did it occur to me we'd have to follow this same route to return from the island when our business finished here. The thought left me bilious, and I imagined myself instead finding a way down to the sea and swimming back to the larger island. Should I leap on purpose, I could avoid those rocks ... The idea, though impractical, offered some relief.

Donall started off, away from the bridge, leaving me no chance to idle. Instead, I watched his form as he walked, watched the strength of his shoulders, and considered the strange fluttering the sight created in my belly. We followed a beaten path through the hills as eventide set in upon us and came to the gates of the ráth even as the guards had begun to close them for the evening. One other thing I had discovered in my time on land: Men did not go outside their forts once the sun set. They feared the Sluagh above all things. Most Men would not venture far from home, and certainly not farther than they could trek in a day, for the wisdom held they must always be behind the closed gates of a ráth before the last rays of the sun winked out. In the night, the Wild Hunt of the Sluagh rode the skies, seeking for souls to claim, or so tales said. I wish I could have asked how walls protected from foes who could fly, but I doubted he could have answered that, regardless.

This place looked older than Dùn Beinn, with earthen foundations built thicker. Yet for all that, still it bore the same general shape. A fortress upon a raised mound, surrounded by a ditch to impede attackers. A bridge spanned the gap, ending in a gate. At first, the guard there brandished an iron spear at our approach, and I tensed. But as we drew nigh, he seemed to recognise my companion. His posture did not grow friendly, but the threat went out of it. "Cutting it close, Donall," he snapped, though he ushered us inside before the gates swung closed behind us.

Those first few nights in Dùn Beinn, I had found it a strange thing, this fear of the night, for merrows are nocturnal by nature. But perhaps the Sluagh would have found us too much trouble to hunt, able to retreat, as we were, into the depths. We, like they, were of Faerie, and thus we did not share Man's fear of it. Or perhaps it would be better to say, we had our own, darker fears of what lurked in the hidden places beyond this world.

The crossbar—iron studded, hateful metal!—that sealed the gates thumped into place, and then someone was escorting us to the chief's great house. Like Donall's home, this one stood in the centre of the town, surrounded by the other wealthy families, with the poorer lots on the outskirts. The walls here looked a mite thicker, the clumps of thatch on the roof more heavily layered, as if the people had greater fear of the weather. Or of the Wild Hunt? Did they think a roof might protect them from a Sluagh?

As we drew nigh to the chief's palace, I mimed once more the babe to Donall, reminding him to inquire about my missing sister. Dahut's memories grew ever more insistent in my mind until I thought I felt the babe's loss as much as she had. I had to find her, for allowing her to remain missing for another day, another hour, it was a barb wedged between my scales. Donall waved my inquiry away, though, lost in the moil of his own thoughts. I huffed in frustration, for without his words, I had no other means to investigate. Being wholly dependent on another to speak for me sat ill with me, and I resolved, one day, to learn the human art of reading and writing.

The Lord of Sgitheanach received us with neither warmth nor hostility. Rather, he sat on a bearskin laid before a low table and bid us join him with a desultory wave. "I thought our business at an end, lad."

Donall had told me, on our journey, that it was in this place the six sons of chiefs had set out, and to here their fathers had come seeking answers. Only with reluctance had Donall revealed it had been Iain to first insist on touching the Kelpie. Though wrathful, the other chiefs had not broken hospitality with the Lord of Sgitheanach to accost either him or Donall.

Donall sat, and I slumped beside him. For a moment, my friend held his peace, then laid a hand on the table. "The chief druid, Donn, called upon us."

"Aye, I'm sure he presses for peace, but not even a druid will deny a father his grief, nor the rage that must accompany it."

Donall was staring at his missing fingers. After a moment, he blew out a long sigh. "Samhain approaches. The druid told me I could breach to the Otherworld, Lord. I could ... save them."

What? What was this madness he spoke of? I slapped the table, drawing the eyes of both men onto me, and stared aghast at my friend. Did he think to descend the Corryvreckan alive? I could not see how any mortal could survive such an attempt, much less hope to return. Besides, I thought it monstrously unlikely the other boys yet lived. Who was this druid, Donn, to propose such absurdity? How did he imagine he could ... Oh. Oh, by the Elder Deep. The druid sought peace at any cost, so he would appease the grieving fathers with the sacrifice of the one they blamed for the loss of their boys. I had seen druids already cast sacrificial victims down to the Kelpie, and this seemed more of the same. And I had no way to explain any of this to Donall. The sheer vexation of that had me wanting to scream; I could scarce manage that, either.

The lord released a pent-up breath. "I think your companion has the right of it, lad. Your plan bespeaks utter madness. What will you do, force the Kelpie to return that which it stole from us? How? At best, this will only serve to offer the one prize that escaped its wrath: you."

Donall cast an angry glance betwixt me and the lord. "I cannot allow my clan to suffer and die because of me."

"So you'll suffer and die for them, and with no guarantee the other clans won't come for claiming what they seek, regardless. Even if you're dead, still it all gives them more than enough reason to take our lands and plunder and apportion it betwixt themselves."

The thought left me queasy. Was I wrong about the druid Donn's reasons, then? Or did he, in his desperation, think to sacrifice Donall for even the faintest hope of peace? Either way, the idea of losing Donall felt akin to chewing off my own arm. I thought I might retch at such a thought.

"None of it will happen if I succeed," Donall protested. He was not looking at me, much though I wished he would. I started to reach for his hand, but fear claimed me, the dread of how he, incensed as he was, might react to the gesture. I could not stand the thought he might pull away from me.

The lord scratched at his brow with this thumb. "Well, I can't stop you from pissing your life away, if you've a mind to do so. But I doubt Iain would have wanted you to walk this fool path."

"If there's any chance he lives ..." Donall said.

But I did not think there was. If only I could have proved it to him.

THE NEXT RÁTH we made for, Dùn Cruinn, lay in the highlands, beside a pristine loch the sight of which had me longing to go for a night swim. I think, if Donall had the least inkling of that idea, he would have flown into a panic at the thought of me being outside the walls at night. Regardless, he remained resolved to his path, and no amount of fervent headshaking, incredulous looks, or attempts to snap him out of his delusions seemed to sway him.

He presented himself to another clan chief and again revealed his plan. I imagine he felt that, if they knew he strove along such lines, they would forestall any plans they made against his father. From the way the lord looked at us, I had my doubts. It did not seem as if he wished to offer us hospitality, but he did so, glowering all the while. The man's other sons kept glaring at us like they wanted to gut us there in middle of their hall. Once, I even saw their father whisper something to cool their nerves. Would it last, though?

The chief granted us a single room, and only that room, even when Donall protested I was a servant and not his wife. The lord claimed the place allotted to us was all they had free, and thus we were given chambers in a tiny room with a dirty hearth pit and flea-ridden blankets.

"It's freezing," Donall said, stoking the fire as best he could, our host having provided us with too little kindling. My friend dragged the mat as close to the hearth as he dared. I recalled Cora's small home and my attempts to stick my fingers into her fire. A few experiments in Donall's hall had broken me of that desire, though the memory had me grinning. Donall plopped down on the mat and looked at me, his head cocked to the side. "I think ... I mean we'll be warmest close together."

I was not certain if the man sought for us to share flesh or just warmth. Either way, I made my way over to him and sat, my back against his chest. Trembling with the chill, he held me close. It was, I think, one of the most content moments of my life. There is a quiet peace found only in the arms of one who cares for you, a warmth more comforting than even the heat of a blazing flame. I wanted to turn, to look in his eyes and see he felt the same. At the same time, I never wanted to move a muscle from this position.

"Why are you so resolved to find the lost princess?" he asked me. And oh! How I longed to answer that. I wanted to tell him everything, even risking he would never believe half of it. I wanted to explain how she was my sister, and, in some way, all this—my sister's abduction, even the fall of Kêr-Ys—might be my fault, as my broken memories of another life told me. I wanted to solve the problems I had caused. But I could no more fix the woes of the land than I could explain any of it.

For almost as long as I could remember, I had been doing things for myself. I could hunt and scavenge. I spent my time scouring sunken ruins for treasure. I knew how to take care of myself ... in my world. In this world, I felt so helpless, and that feeling chafed more than any saddle-soreness. That thought pushed the breath from my chest, stole the joy I had, a moment earlier, seized upon in finding myself held close to his chest.

I twisted around until I could stare into his eyes, willing him to understand. But I had no such power to share my thoughts, and in the end, we slept, wrapt in each other's arms against the bitter cold. And slowly, in that embrace, my gloom seeped out of me. When I was certain he slept, I laid my palm against his cheek.

"WE NEED some supplies afore we head further," Donall told me in the morn. So we went into the town, and he set to haggling with merchants for what we'd need to reach our next stop. Though I looked to the merchants some, I found my interest pulled by the gossip of the market. I kept thinking, somehow, someone might mention something about my sister or where she might have gotten off to.

The square was crowded, overflowing in my eyes, with people and stalls, with smells and sounds. Vendors hawked furs from wolf or bear or skins from deer or rabbit, and I ogled them, unfamiliar with many of these creatures, wondering what they had looked like in life. Other men called out to sell eggs or vegetables or sundry house goods like firewood or lamp oil. There were shops jammed so close together that people shouted overtop one another in their cries for attention, and I pitied them, if their lives depended on striving so hard to compel others to their places. There were women, I saw, who beckoned men into alleys beyond the market, and I wondered what goods they sold in those hidden places, and why they did not display their wares like other merchants. There were carts with cages full of squawking chickens, which a vendor promised me "laid an egg nigh every morn." Just at the market's edge, I saw a man dealing in small, grumpy horses I had earlier learnt were called donkeys. Whilst I thought horses regal, after I found I disliked the stench and mewling noises donkeys made, I decided not to show them to Donall, lest he decide he wanted one for a new mount. I thought his horse, Haggis, a noble animal, with a noble name, and one I would not like to see challenged by a donkey.

As I was looking around, I spotted the chief's sons as they crept up on Donall, clubs in hand. Before they could reach him, I seized my friend's hand and, just as one of the assailants struck, yanked him aside. Donall yelped but quickly recovered and shoved me behind him, fists raised. I ducked around, intercepting the other brother, who tried to close in behind Donall.

The man lunged for my friend, but I caught his wrist. The chief's son screwed up his face, perhaps shocked I had manhandled him, or perhaps enraged. Either way, he'd intended to hit Donall in the head, which might well have killed my dearest companion. The man tried to jerk his arm free, but his strength was no match for the might of a merrow. The rage that took me then had none of the flavour of blood frenzy. Rather, it was a dark, bitter thing—indignation that this young man thought to murder my friend. I twisted his arm until I felt joints pop and bones crack. The boy fell wailing to his knees, clutching his arm, and I left him to his misery.

By the time I turned back, Donall had overpowered the other attacker, taken the club and left his foe lying in the street with a bloody lip. "Best we be gone from here before more trouble finds us," he said.

I could not have agreed more.

AFTER A STOP back at Dùn Beinn, we headed south, toward the shoreline. "Mynydd y Gaer lies nigh to where the isthmus of Kêr-Ys once stood. The isthmus is all part of the strait now, and on either side of it, I have ... Well, I once had friends. From here, our last stop will require us to sail across the strait to reach Bro Érech."

The name tickled something in my memory, but I could not quite place it. Not at first.

Mynydd y Gaer lay both along the strait and at the mouth of a river running from distant mountains. It was a centre of trade, the largest we had yet come to. It sat atop a tall hill, the plateau-like summit ringed by a stone wall I imagined would have protected the place. Such defences existed more to ward against other Men than Sluagh, I decided. Archers stood atop the wooden ramparts that mounted the stone foundations, watching us as we approached. Within, we were met by knights who escorted us to meet the king of these lands.

On the way, Donall had warned me that Iain and he had made a cattle raid in these lands, some years back, and the death of their prince, Rhys, would not have made matters any better. As he predicted, we found our welcome only a hair warmer than what we'd gotten in the highlands. At least until Donall explained his plan about the Kelpie. Then, I saw light kindled in King Dafydd's eyes, a frenzied desperation to believe. This one, I thought, would have traded all he had to have his son back. Dafydd would have made peace in a heartbeat to regain his boy. But since Rhys was no doubt dead, would it make the man all the worse a foe when he realised his hopes were made of sand?

I feared for what he would do and what he would make Donall and his people suffer when he saw what I saw.

At my behest, Donall took to asking around the town about the lost princess of Ys. He consulted druids and bards with me following, and we heard a half dozen different tales. Some claimed she was long dead. Others said the Wild Hunt had taken her to Falias. Or a different Sluagh had absconded with her to the Enchanted Forest where she lived in a hut that walked on chicken legs. Or an evil sorceress had carried her off to Starfall Vale, and she was wandering in the mist. One bard claimed the princess grew up in the lost city of the ogres, somewhere in the Ogre-peaks. We had no way to know if any of the tales had the least kernel of truth to them, but I refused to give it over.

In the night, I awakened to the sounds of the most mournful song imaginable. It was faint, far off, as though ferried to me on a soughing wind. Something about it pricked my soul like the needles that abused my feet, and I scrambled to the window and threw wide the shutters. A heavy fog had rolled in during the night, and I couldn't see the stars. The song seemed to come from the direction of the water, though.

Standing there, hung half over the windowsill, I heard them call my name. *Lí Ban, Lí Ban, Lí Ban* ... My sisters knew I was here and they grieved for me. Their song was a threnody to lament my passing from their world. My heart broke, then, as shattered as the ruins of Kêr-Ys, both taken by the sea.

I gasped, couldn't breathe, and slumped against the windowsill. Home beckoned to me, offered me the—false—hope I could return to the world I had known all my life. The desire to slip back into the familiar slithered upon me like some hidden eel, already wrapt around my body ere I knew it lurked nigh. I had left *everything* behind that day, had cast aside all that made me who I was, every tie to my kin and very nature, because me obsession with Men and my dreams of another life had, at the time, seemed more pressing. The distant, unclaimable desire had felt so much deeper than aught I already had within my grasp, so I tossed all I had aside to speed after a chance for something new.

I was lost, so lost I could no longer see my hands before my face, could scarce picture even the destination I had sought. Had I, swept up in the moment, in the burning desire in my breast, dived into something without the least consideration, the least preparation for what I would find in those foreign depths? Aye, well I knew I had, and borne upon the wind of that sound, that acknowledgment gouged me like obsidian blades, flensed the heart out of me. I no longer knew myself, no longer knew my own body, even, scarce knew this world I found myself in. The weight of such a revelation crushed me, and I slipped to my knees against the windowsill.

Mererid ... I moaned, within my own mind, unable to call to her. Not only would Donall never voice my name, but I would never again speak the names of my kin, of anyone. I would not speak of her, to her. Would not swim beside her, laughing as we danced amid pods of dolphins, or hiding in reefs. We would not race along the shadows, beneath silver moonlight, nor sit upon rocks and comb our hair. Her voice was so close I could almost reach out, could almost grasp it. But, no, it might as well have come from the empty spaces betwixt the stars, so unreachable had it become.

Shivering in the cool night air, unable to see a damn thing for the fog, I wept. Tears streamed down my cheeks, and I lost myself in mutual grief with my kindred. For I knew I would not see them again, and I had no way to join my voices to theirs as we had done so oft in days gone.

I had gained all I ever sought—save the missing princess—and I had to account those gains worth the trade. I had to, for if I allowed myself to wallow in what I had lost, it would drown me. And kneeling there, in the depths of my grief and burgeoning self-pity, I saw his face in my mind. More than aught else imaginable, I needed to see him now.

Ere I could stop myself I rose—tears still streaming down my face—and stumbled from my room, coming to the adjacent chamber Dafydd had given Donall. I knew, sometimes, Men locked their doors, and for an instant, I feared that would be the case. But when I tried the door, it gave way, opening into the man's chamber. His shutters remained ajar, letting a silver band of moonlight spill into the room, offering more than enough light for my merrow eyes. He lay on his side, gently snoring, blissfully unaware I had intruded into his space, even as he remained unaware I, a fae, had intruded into his world.

I leant against the doorjamb, watching him, my tears slowly abating, my breaths becoming regular once more. My sisters' song had ripped me apart, left me raw and bleeding. But within that sundered mess of me, still I had something. Aye, I had left behind a world, but I had gained a new one.

And though I would never sing again, would never see my sisters again, I was not alone. My choice had been sudden, but it had been a choice, the chance to move toward what mattered most to me. I thought, then, every choice must always come with a price, every gain bought with the loss of some other possibility. Surely, then, 'twas better to move through life with volition than be swept along by tides. I had made a choice, and that alone meant I was stronger than most, stronger even than I had accounted myself ere now. Choices were pain, aye, but too, they created the meaning of our lives.

So I watched his face, the fluttering of his eyelids, as I wondered what dreams played out there. In the regularity of his breathing, I stilled the wild pounding of my heart. I need not sing if, in place of what I had lost, I had gained something better.

❦

WE TOOK a ship across the strait and, standing at the gunwale, Donall looked to me while I watched the passing waves. "I am not giving up on the princess, foundling. Rather, I needs must make the peace work first. Besides, mayhap I can make the Kelpie tell me ... I don't know. Tell me something of account."

I rolled my eyes at that, though I'm not certain he saw. The Kelpie would not aid him. That spirit would do naught save take something else from me. Once, I had thought the spirit placing me so nigh to Donall a mercy. Now, I began to suspect it was a perverse cruelty—to place what I needed in view, but forever out of reach. By taking my voice, the Kelpie knew I would fail. I had lost my home, my body, all I had known, and still not gained what I sought. But I would prove him wrong. I would make Donall love me ... and not only because such was my bargain. No, the truth was, somewhere along this route, *I* had fallen for him. And I would not allow the Kelpie to claim either of us.

I thought of how my sisters had come singing for me in the night. To have heard them here meant they must have been swimming over the ruins of the sunken city I had so loved. They had come so close for me, and thinking about it in the light of day, I was no longer certain they could have known where I was. Perhaps they oft came here to sing for me. Perhaps they had no idea where I had gone, could never have imagined I would have bargained with the Kelpie as I had done. I had wronged them, leaving without a word. It was another misdeed I had no way to make up for, and they might spend the rest of their lives wondering what had befallen me. Had I fallen prey to a shark or a rival merrow clan? Had I gotten lost in the vastness of the sea? Had I, in my reckless curiosity, wakened some Old One serpent from the depths and been swallowed whole?

They would never know my fate, and I would never know their minds. That thought burrowed through me like a gnawing worm, eating away my guts, threatening to devour my very heart. I had longed for this life more than aught in the World ... but the cost! The cost of a thing, perhaps, can only be truly understood once paid.

But I would not allow myself to dwell on that. Last night, I had resolved to push forward, and I would hold myself toward it, redirecting my wavering heart whenever it should falter. I must.

Bro Érech proved to be more of a city than the ráths of Inis Fáil, though it was tiny compared to the massive ruins of Kêr-Ys. The city abutted a small bay, which gave shelter to ships come to moor, like our own. After the ship was tied down, I followed Donall over the gangplank and into the harbour, a place bustling with people and redolent with the scents of fish and brine. The smells had my stomach growling. I could almost imagine poor Donall's face should I grab a cod and take a bite, a thought that had me grinning.

No, I would have to wait for him to introduce us to our host and hope they provided fresh food.

"Bleiz," Donall told me as we made our way to the lord's hall, "my friend the Kelpie took. He was the younger son of the late King Gwezenneg. His brother, Mael, I hear he reigns as king of Bro Érech now, though for many years their mother was the queen regent."

I wanted to ask how, unlike the other clan chiefs we had visited, these southern ones took the name of king. I still knew so very little of the politics of the surface world, and Nemedia seemed a complex nest of interwoven dependencies. How much damage had been done to the Kingdoms of Man by my failings as Dahut, I would never know. Oh, how I wished I could recall the cloudy details of my past life. Instead, I remained mired in guilt for mistakes I could not quite recall.

Bro Érech was denser than any of the ráths, with buildings that seemed eager to climb overtop one another, spreading like barnacles. A thick aroma of human waste and refuse wafted out of every alley we passed as we threaded our way through the main thoroughfare. Too, I had to watch my step from a handful of horse droppings left in steaming piles hither and thither.

There was beauty and vibrance—with brightly dyed cloths attracting my eye to many a stall—but a foulness too, to this place, as if the people and animals behind these walls had been forced into too small a space. As if they had forgotten they were choking on their own filth.

Would Kêr-Ys too have felt thus, had I seen it outside of dream? Would all its wonder have seemed smeared by these faults? Mayhap I was fortunate to look upon only the ruin and imagine the grandeur, free of grime or the spreading cracks that must rive the foundations. For now, seeing Bro Érech, I thought I preferred the smaller ráths of Inis Fáil, where a person could breathe and walk without being jostled, could still feel themselves part of the Earth.

Perhaps sensing my unease, Donall took my hand and helped me navigate the crowded streets until we came, at last, to the king's palace. It was a wooden castle, three storeys high and festooned with banners. I caught Donall casting a glance my way, perhaps expecting me to stand in awe, for here lay the finest building he had yet brought me to. Did his regard rest on my face overlong? I thought perhaps it had ... Of course, I had grown up in a palace of glistening coral, in a city of amber. Whilst I found the palace before me interesting for what it told me of life among Men—how they worked, how they revelled in ordering about others, how they ate, slept, and loved—I was hardly speechless at the construction. Nevertheless, I allowed a naïve smile to spread across my face, for I knew he wanted to see it through my eyes, and thus sample some vicarious joy in these trying times. I knew now, despite the pain that lanced my feet, I would have walked the length of the continent to see his smile. I would have fought sea serpents or dragons to shelter him. And slowly, the realisation came to my heart that, when he went to challenge the Kelpie, I would go with him. I would die beside him ere I let him face danger alone.

I had found the love the Kelpie had challenged me to find, only, I could not see it reflected in his eyes. Not yet. Still, I had to believe the friendship he saw in me could bloom into more, given time and proximity. And sometimes, sometimes, I felt his touch on my hand linger, giving me hope. I could not tell him how I felt, but he would see, day by day. This I told myself with each painful step as we entered the palace.

We were greeted by the king's seneschal, who escorted us to the main hall. Several men stood there, peering down at a picture sketched in ash upon an animal hide. I could not get a good glimpse of it and wondered what could so fascinate these men. One I took as a leader among them, for he wore a golden torc.

"King Mael," Donall addressed him with a bowed head. Tension held my friend's posture stiff as stones. I judged this King Mael the strongest of all those we had called upon, though the most removed on account of the distance.

The man addressed stared long at Donall, his expression impassive, save for a dangerous glint in his eyes. It was the sort of look an eel has the instant before it lunges. The king was, I thought, at most ten years senior to Donall, with sandy hair and a drooping, oiled moustache. His bare arms bore whorling tattoos that reminded me of a thick thread, woven back upon itself, over and over, in an endless loop. "Why have you come, islander? I did not send for you."

"No one sent for me, aye," Donall admitted. "Yet I come to you in the pursuit of peace." He pointed a hand at the picture on the table. "And here I find you poring over maps of my lands."

Mael folded his arms over his chest and stared hard at Donall. "The map shows all the lands running both sides of the strait, including my own. If you see threat in that, perhaps it is your guilty conscience, islander."

"My conscience didn't sketch out the location of Dùn Beinn."

The king shrugged. "As you like it. I'll give it to you true, then. My father sought to be a king free of Kêr-Ys, and now I am that. I doubt even he imagined, though, the chance to be a new High King, and yet here we are. Gralon and all his line are gone. The High blood has run dry, and now comes the chance for whoever proves strongest to unite the pieces of Nemedia. Before the mountain of such ambition, Dùn Beinn is but a pebble. It shall be added to the mound or kicked aside, as seems best at the time."

I had not thought it possible for Donall to grow stiffer yet. "Pebbles can cause a great deal of woe if you go kicking them about. They get stuck in your sandal, and next you know, you're leaving bloody footprints in your wake."

"And yet, in the end, it remains but an annoyance to be plucked out and discarded."

"Brother," a woman's voice said, and we all turned to see her stride into the light, azure gown flowing about her like lapping waves. I knew her. She was the one from the Fane of Teutates, who had nursed Donall back to health.

"Faoinèis ..." Donall gasped, then looked back to Mael. "*Brother*? You're the princess of Bro Érech?"

"Aye." She bowed. "But do not think I deceived you, back when I was apprenticed at the fane. It was not as though you ever said the names of those who perished at your side, nor had I seen Bleiz in some time. I'd no idea of the foolish endeavour the two of you took."

"Oh, 'twas at my behest," Mael admitted. "Had we found the princess of Ys, war might have proved needless to secure my position as High King. Bleiz was all too happy to recruit his friends to hunt for the lass." He shook his head, looking somewhat put out. "I sent you to find a girl and you tried to claim a gods-damned horse, and a cursed one at that. I don't blame you for his death, but neither do I have much use for you, islander."

"Brother," Faoinèis said again. "At least offer them hospitality for a few days after they have come so far. You cannot claim a throne by discarding all civility."

I imagine I too have worn such a long-suffering look as he now favoured his sister with. Perhaps all siblings reserve such expressions only for one another. "So be it. I leave them in your care, and if you wish, you may arrange a feast for tomorrow night. Let it not be said that I am not a generous king."

After a nod at her brother, Faoinèis led us from the main hall and down a corridor. "So, who is this companion of yours?"

Donall glanced my way for the first time since the druid woman had appeared, but his regard was fleeting before he turned back to her, and my face burned from the slight. He had a past with this woman, thought she had saved him—*my actions saved him!*—and now, in her presence, he barely afforded me a moment's thought? "My servant and travelling companion."

His callous answer plunged into my gut like the prongs of a bone trident, twisting, shredding my insides. Was that all I was to him? Even now? Even after ... But how, for I was certain I had felt his stolen glances toward me before, the lingering of his hand upon mine, the closeness of our bodies, our hearts. And all of that amounted to dust the moment Faoinèis showed her face.

"Has she a name?"

"Without doubt, but as a mute foundling, I have not been able to discover it." I frowned, feeling once more slighted, though I could not think of aught he said that was not true. "How did I not know you were a princess?" Donall blurted. "I spent days in convalescence in your care. Now I think I did not know you at all."

She snorted. "You knew me as a druid. Did you imagine a person is only one thing, and that you would know all they were from a few encounters? Besides, you were in a hurry to make for home and report your tragedy, and my family—I thought—had no bearing on your plight. Why would I bring up my brothers?" She opened a door and revealed a guest chamber which she gave to Donall, who retired to rest.

Down the hall, Faoinèis showed me a much plainer room I could use. After I entered and tossed my bag on the floor, the druid woman lingered on the threshold, watching me. I had the unnerving feeling her eyes raked beneath my flesh, as if poring over my soul. Predators look at prey thus, and I wanted to claw her eyes out. I imagined seizing her, crushing her spine. Feasting on her flesh until not even bone remained ...

No! Never had I tasted Man-flesh as a merrow, I would surely not let the blood frenzy take me here, when I had become almost human.

"Mute?" she asked. I nodded. "So, no way to tell us of your past, then." She clucked her tongue. "That's ... unfortunate."

I spread my hands. I had little inclination to try to explain aught to this woman. She had done a service in saving Donall, and perhaps in getting Mael to offer us hospitality too. Yet somehow I found I took an instant disliking to her. Perhaps I disliked how Donall seemed with her. Never before had I seen him so flustered, and it left me feeling queasy and disconsolate.

"Well," Faoinèis said, "take some rest then. We serve supper later."

I nodded and flopped down on the mat before me.

IN THE EVENING, we took supper with King Mael and his retinue. It was too cold to eat in the yard, so instead we sat in a fume-choked hall, warmed by braziers that stank of burning oils. The scents of roasted pork mingled with those of smoke and unwashed bodies and heady aromas of wine. I found my senses taken by an onslaught that further darkened my already dour mood, and I pictured myself dashing from this over-crowded hall and running back down to the harbour. I imagined diving into the icy water and swimming the strait, seeking for the sisters who had come singing for me the night before. Would they come again? Could I find them?

Donall remained distracted, scarcely saying two words to me. I took solace in the bite of wine, which our host provided in ample portions. I wish I could say the drink smothered my dolours, but in truth, it merely allowed me to sink into the trench of them and wallow in my misery. The numbness of wine spread from limbs to heart, and I sat sullen, only half listening to the conversations droning in the hall.

King Mael bragged over how grand a feast he would throw on the morrow, of the giving of gifts and troughs of wine and food to make the gods themselves envious. I found myself dubious about such claims. In other circumstances, I would have leapt at the chance to see a feast among Men, for it promised to be a grand celebration. But the distance between myself and Donall felt like pieces of my flesh were being ripped from me, a torment drawn out slow, by the cruellest of foes. After another swig of wine, I resolved to fight back against that tormentor. If I wanted things to change for the better between my friend and me, I would have to change them.

Samhain drew nigh upon us and I needed to reach him before he could make his ill-fated attempt against the Kelpie. I would show him my heart and then dare to hope he could see an alternative to his suicidal plan to reclaim lost souls. This, I swore to myself, I would do the moment we were away from this hateful place and alone once more.

FATHER REFUSED TO ACT, caught in the brambles of grief, deluded by idealistic hope. As if peace could endure in the face of treachery. As if a price did not come due.

Only a hint of a trail before me, barely visible in the torchlight, but I knew the way.

A moonless night. A time of peril, when good folk would hide behind iron-barred doors. I was not them now, if ever I had been.

I walked through the darkened wood, my hood thrown back, a basket of flowers on my arm. In the distance, wolves were howling. Scents of loam and petrichor made the forest seem fresh, mocking the darkness of my heart. A faint rumble of thunder crackled somewhere far away. I cast a glance skyward—wondered if the Wild Hunt rode—though I could see naught through the canopy. I would not fear, not that. Not this night.

Bodies without heads. Souls in agony, caught betwixt this world and the other.

Onward, along the rough path. I should not be here, had to be.

Before me, the nemeton opened, centred around the great oak, fallen now. Lightning blasted, its stump a husk. A memory. An altar, long used in days—nights—when a certain operation became needful.

I paced the periphery of the slight clearing. The oak, it had been massive, thicker around than my arm span. Its roots ran wide, grasping and choking through the soil. It had prevented other trees from growing too nigh this place, had created something sacred. Sacred to Cernunnos, aye. I wouldn't dare evoke such a powerful god, though. Not for this.

Sometimes, wretchedness, wickedness became the only course.

Bodies without heads. And her, a sister, missing, lost. As if I would permit a knife to hover forever a hair above her throat.

My skin prickled and I rubbed my arms. It was not the chill of the night. I had the distinct sensation of gazes upon my back, watching me, waiting to see what I would do. If my courage would break. Almost, I could see two disembodied heads, one male, one female, gazing at me through the foliage. A mother, a brother, spurring me onward.

Bodies without heads. Heads without bodies. Souls without rest.

A haunting, damning refrain playing through my mind, teasing me with inchoate images on the fringes of my vision. Almost there, almost I saw them, watchful.

I knelt before the altar, smoothed the ashes in the stump's hollow. The wood was almost petrified. The centre had seen so many offerings made here, over years, over centuries. Another head, once, I had heard, burnt here. I would not go that far. Prayed I never needed to go that far.

Some said, Creiddylad herself had blessed this oak, when it lived. A sacred nemeton, aye. The Earth thrummed with pain, here; in times, cruelty was warranted, sacrifice needful. I had learnt well, for I had always proved an apt pupil.

I wedged my torch into the loam, then emptied my basket, spreading the rapunzel flowers across the offering bed. A breeze set the leaves soughing, had me casting about. I saw only the darkness, and it was vast, encroaching upon me like giant fingers closing. Ready to engulf me. Ready to welcome me into its gloom. A place prepared for me unless I turned back.

Bodies without heads.

My breath caught in my throat. I was choking, gasping, almost ready to break into weeping. Not again, not now. "I have not come for tears," I told myself. Leastwise, not my tears.

Blood for blood, and pain for pain.

I took up my torch, touched it to the flowers, watched them curl and char. Tendrils wafted skyward, vanished into the dark overhead. "Black Annis, Black Annis ..." I chanted, struggling to keep my voice steady, struggling not to falter, given my rising panic. "'Neath a moonless night I call you. Black Annis, Black

Annis, in the hour of wolves I summon you. Black Annis, Black Annis, from the shadows come."

I sliced my palm, flung droplets of blood onto the burning flowers, for blood called between the worlds.

"Black Annis, Black Annis, heed my call and let the empty darkness be filled with your glory."

In truth, I did not know for certain this would work. I did not know if she would respond, or how long it would take. A time I sat on my knees, waiting, looking about. Praying she would come, hoping she would not.

Chill sweats and shaking palms. I should have run, should have fled. Could not back down now.

Leaves rustled behind me, bushes disturbed. I leapt to my feet. Spun. There, amid the undergrowth, she stood, a bare silhouette in the darkness, shrouded by a blood-red cloak. She was a little woman, much shorter than me, and yet her presence filled the grove. Something vast. Something ... monstrous in scope. Like seeing a protruding root and knowing you saw only a tiny vestige of the whole.

"What would you have?" the Other asked.

No turning back. Never any turning back. Heads without bodies. A missing babe. "Vengeance. I want to see Gwezenneg brought low for all he has done. I want to see him writhe in agony before he dies. I want to bring my sister home, alive and safe."

"I will have your treasure."

A price, always, of course. What matter silver or gold next to blood? "As much as you can carry," I assured her.

From within her red cloak, the Other produced a phial, held it out to me. No claws, despite the tales. Just fingers, just the tiny hand, as of a girl. "Drink, before you get to him. All his deep cunning shall be overshadowed beneath the rising mountain of his lust." Not what I had wished for, but it would do. It meant I would look into his eyes as I killed him. I said that, said I wanted to see him brought low. In her other hand, she offered a second phial. "When it is done, drink this one, and eyes shall slide over you, like water flowing around river stones. You will walk free from his castle, ride from there."

Because I said I wanted to bring my sister home. A slow smile crept over my face as I realised my well-chosen words had ensured my success. Always, the elders warned against bargaining with the Others, said to choose our words with care. But it was not so hard as that; not so hard.

I took both phials, careful to keep them separated. The Other stepped back, vanished into the darkness, the last I saw, a glimpse of her red riding hood. Gone, gone.

And I had places to be.

＆

THE NEXT DAY, I saw very little of Donall, as he took counsel with Mael, no doubt striving for peace. I passed the time wandering the city, though careful not to travel so far I could not make my way back to the palace. It towered over the rest of the buildings, making it an easy enough landmark, and I had a fair sense of direction. I longed to go back down to the harbour, but I feared that path might prove too far.

Alone, I felt strangely abandoned by my friend. Since coming into his care, I had scarcely found myself apart from him for more than a few hours, at least in daylight. In this strange, foreign city, I had naught on which to tether myself, especially not without him at my side. Always, he had led the way, guided me through crowds, made certain I kept safe against the myriad perils of urban life. When he spoke, his voice cut the drone of the thousand others. My soul ached to feel cast adrift here, and I milled one way or the next, acutely aware it little mattered where I wandered. Maybe that hurt more—the thought that I could go wherever suited me, and not a person would care. Here, I was alone.

The city seemed somewhat different to those on Inis Fáil, with taller buildings, jammed up against one another as though someone had shoved people shoulder to shoulder. White walls were banded by wooden boards, often in alternating or crossing patterns I found fascinating. Sometimes, the eaves of higher floors overhung the streets. Oft, in these situations, people had shops on the ground floors, with what I took for dwellings above those. When there was space between buildings, those spaces were so narrow a large man could scarce pass through without turning to the side. I traced my fingers along borders and mortars, vaguely curious, though the mortal world no longer held so much of the wonder as once it had. I tried to tell myself my desultoriness stemmed from my growing familiarity with the land, though I knew my malaise had more to do with a certain female druid.

When the city failed to hold my interest, I listened to conversations, ever seeking news of the lost princess of Kêr-Ys. But years had passed, and I think the fallen city was less and less on people's minds. Now, they spoke of the coming festivals, or of the war that would no doubt impend when spring returned. They chatted over their banalities, even while, in my mind, I screamed for someone to tell me where to find my missing sister.

So the day waned, and I returned to Mael's castle for the feast. Donall saw me and beckoned me to his side with a warm smile. Warmer than he'd managed since we'd come to Bro Érech, and my heart leapt. I pantomimed a ship sailing on the sea, hoping we would be gone from here in the morn.

"You want to go sailing?" he asked. "Perhaps we can soon. The ruins of Kêr-Ys would lie just within that strait. So much history, all just drowned. Or maybe it waits down there, silent as a dream."

I did not know what to make of his wistful musings about Kêr-Ys. What did a ruin he'd never laid eyes on matter to him? Still, I wished I could show it to him, as I had seen it, diving its meandering halls, exploring the length of its broken facade.

There were platters of steaming boar and whole roasted pigs spread across the tables. There were trays with sweat breads, I wished I could have tasted more, given how the other ladies seemed to savour them. Too, there was roasted cod and bass, and to these I gravitated. Since losing both my tongue and my shark-teeth—having to rely on weak, dull human ones now—I found eating more chore than joy. Still, I found some comfort in dining on fish, for the familiarity of it.

More, there was wine, and though I could not taste much of that either, I could feel its warm bite and the comfort it brought. I took to dipping bread in my cup, making it sodden enough each bite was easy to chew and swallow.

King Mael sat in the centre of all the feasting, in the middle of the great table. His arms and fingers glittered in the firelight, so bedecked was he in gold and silver. It was an ostentatious display of his wealth, I assumed, yet every so often, some knight or other would come as he called. The king would welcome the man, perhaps embrace him, then remove a piece of his jewellery and hand it to the petitioner. Were these the fabled gifts he had spoken of the night prior?

It struck me he was buying friendship with these people. Was there not something crass in all that? But the guests received their awards with such earnest gratitude, I began to think it more ritual than bribe.

At last, the king called Donall, using my friend's name for the first time I had heard. I had not even realised he knew his name, for ere now he'd always been "islander," and naught more. But now Mael embraced him. When he released my beloved, Mael raised a hand high, and the hall quieted. Raucous laughter and rumbling conversations shushed, becoming faint murmurs on the fringes of the hall.

It was then I noticed Faoinèis lurking nearby. The druid woman smiled at Donall, but after a moment, her gaze settled on me, sharp as a blade. Sick foreboding grew in my gut. Merrow instinct warned me of peril, bid me spring into preemptive violence and tear out her throat.

"In the name of peace," Mael said, "my sister will wed Donall of Dùn Beinn and thus join our families!"

A cheer went up, echoing in the rafters, and goblets beat against the table. Hands clapped, men whooped, and cups were thrown back to drain their contents in single swigs.

And I ... I sat there aghast, unable to believe what I had just heard. For all at once, the future I had seen shattered to pieces against a rocky shore. And I would lose everything. Even my very *soul*. The moment he bound himself to Faoinèis, I was destroyed. I would lose not only the man I loved but *myself*. I would perish and be drawn down to the Kelpie, his prey.

At last, too late, bleeding out where I sat, I apprehended the invisible blade the druid woman had held at my throat. With one swift stroke, she had taken from me everything I ever wanted, everything I could ever have. My mouth flapped like a flounder tossed ashore, trying to suck down breaths I could never take, for I had been cast into a foreign world, where even the air was poison to me. On my forearms, I leant against the table, unable to stop the meaningless flapping of my mouth. I knew the druid cast her vicious, sidelong glances at me. I knew Donall did not see me at all—had, it seemed, *never* seen me, much though I had let myself believe he knew me best.

At that moment, I would have cut off my own tail flukes to escape such a trap. But there was no way out. I had willingly swum into this darkness, and I could never find my way free of it.

INTERLUDE: DAHUT

The vast vestibule of the Golden Castle remained unlit, almost pitch black in the rising twilight. Dahut could see, on the floor by the door, more gold tracery inlaid into the stonework. Past that, she could make out little else. The darkness had a weight to it, as if the shadows were not just an absence of light, but a mass, looming, watching her.

She knelt, fished through her satchel, and withdrew a torch. It took several tries to spark it before the oil-soaked rag caught, spewing forth its acrid stench. Now, torchlight glinted off the gold filigree that striated every stone in the vestibule. It sent the well of shadows leaping for the darkened recesses of the vaulting ceiling and left the castle a glittering, eerie vision. Dreamlike. And perilous. For like dreams, she had the sense this place could shift around her, inchoate and mercurial. That the rules of the world she knew no longer applied. Here, reality became something altogether other.

Her footfalls, though faint, sounded clomping and inelegant on the marmoreal floor, echoing through the hall as she made her way forward. She held the torch high, behind her head so as not to ruin her night vision, and slowly turned about, taking the measure of this place. Arcing buttresses supported a great dome, the architecture unlike aught built by Man. Indeed, the only thing she had ever seen to compare was the Smith

Lord's masterwork, her own city of Kêr-Ys. But where his creation stood strong against the encroaching of time, this golden castle was riddled with cracks, a fading wonder of a bygone age.

If there was a king here, he ruled an empty hall and oversaw a land without subjects, attended by none save the stones and the mountain winds. What would drive the wizard to dwell here, alone? Here, he shunned the company of Mankind and the Others, both. Here, the solitude loomed as thick as the shadows.

At the end of the hall lay curving double staircases, framing an alcove. The stairs rose up to the balcony that rimmed the vestibule, where she would perhaps find the wizard, Rumpelstiltskin. Within the alcove lay a quiescent fountain, its rim rived with cracks that ensured it would never again hold water. At the fountain's heart lay a broken statue, only the legs remaining, those belonging to a nude woman.

Something about it sat ill with her and she whirled from it, hurrying up the left stairway. She had taken leave of her senses coming here, she knew now. But there was naught for it save to press on; she could not well leave and face the night outside, on the mountainside. Yet, the sense of rising dread increased with each step she took toward the balcony until she hesitated on the landing, suddenly short of breath. She cast about, turning the torch one way and the next. The shadows shifted, recoiled as the light brushed close. The dark seemed to whisper ... something. Not words, not that she could make out. More like the susurrations of the leaves, if such could have carried intent. Could have carried wakefulness. Aye, that was it, the castle seemed to be waking, and with that thought, her palms grew clammy. A cold sweat trickled down her back, as if she had needed further reminder of her folly in crossing the Albia.

"I am the whirlwind," she whispered.

But she could not shake the sense that the shadows laughed at her.

Still, she pushed on, for before her opened a wide corridor, beckoning. A crack in the ceiling allowed a silver band of moonlight to illumine the centre of the hall. Dahut's steps were slower now as she tried to muffle the sound of her boots. She passed forward, through the beam of light, beyond which the dark redoubled, gathering in every corner. Like a swarm of rats, watching her passage. But whichever way she turned her torch, she saw no sign of life, no sign of aught. Her mind played tricks on her, was all. More than that she refused to countenance.

At the end of the corridor, a tall archway led into a great hall. More gold-banded doors had once sectioned off the hall, but now one lay in a decaying pile on the ground, the other hanging on by a single, warped hinge. Dahut eased herself through, having to duck a little to avoid touching the rotting door.

"Come, come, then," a soft male voice called from the back of the hall, and Dahut started, jerking the torch up. Its light did not reach far enough to reveal the speaker.

By all the gods of Man, she wanted to flee from this place. Instead, she pushed forward until her torchlight at last fell upon the figure who reclined on his throne. Sprawled on it, rather, for he dangled one leg over an armrest, leaning against the other, his own spindly arm at an odd angle behind his head. The figure was shorter than her, and thin enough to look sickly, even not accounting for the paleness of his flesh. His throne was carved, seemingly from a single gigantic hunk of gold, wrought in fine detail, decorated with intricate spirals.

"Hehe," he said. "Come to gawk at the King of the Golden Mountain, have we? Heh. Well, take a look and see if he's to your liking."

This creature, Man or Other, had taken payment from Dahut's mother in flesh. That knowledge lent a lascivious tinge to his regard and had her skin crawling. Even so, she continued to advance on the enthroned figure. "You are the wizard Rumpelstiltskin?"

The figure shrugged. "Mmm. I've gone by that name, time to time. Deliciously absurd, yes, and she thought it my *name*." His voice had a musical quality to it, but it was the music of rising tension, of something dire impending. He licked his lips. "And you, fair one, are the princess Dahut, daughter of Gralon and Dieub." He did not say that he had known her mother. He did not need to.

There was an alienness to this creature, much akin to what she'd felt in meeting Black Annis. Yes, Dahut was certain now, she dealt with someone Other. A timelessness marked his features, like looking at a mountain, and knowing it had seen the passing of ages before you gawped at it, knowing it would see more after you were dust. Like a mountain, like the sea, such a sempiternal force was a part of the world, and its thoughts must needs move in strange revolutions unknowable to a Man.

"Where is my sister? Where are the *both* of them?" she corrected herself. "The one you took, so long ago, where is she?" Dahut had not intended to ask over the other girl, and yet now, standing here, she had to.

"Ooo. Sleeping, yes." The creature sucked air between his teeth. "Not of your father's divine blood, that one. Still, such a beauty, my sweet darling."

That girl would have been Dahut's older sister, and of a sudden, a great longing to see her came over Dahut. But such was not why she'd come, and her mother had willingly surrendered that child, long back. "And can you tell me where Black Annis took my baby sister?"

"Eh ... I could tell you how to find her, I could." The wizard shrugged. "But what reward is in it for me, spiting that vengeful one? A deal, mayhap?" He leant forward, drumming his fingertips together. "Deal?"

His eyes glinted in the torchlight, darkly luminous. She wanted to turn from him, couldn't. This was why she had come. She had crossed Nemedia and beyond for this. This creature, wretched, aye, but needful in her desperation. "What deal?"

"Your birthright, Princess, on behalf of my daughter, my sweet, beauty."

Dahut blanched. She wanted to flee then. He asked too much. All her life, she had been the eldest born, the true heir of Kêr-Ys, and the throne had been her destiny. Even now, even knowing she had an elder half-sister ... They shared her mother's blood, but not the royal line of her father. If anyone knew the truth of her bastard parentage, her sister would never have been in line for the crown. This was Dahut's and Dahut's alone.

"Not quite ready to sacrifice so very much, then?" Again, she could not help but note the perverse music of his words, almost sung to her. "Don't want the babe back that badly?"

Dahut set her jaw. What would she give to fix this? The missing babe was her sister, and Dahut would do whatever it took to see her safe, see her returned home. Even if it meant surrendering her own birthright to a half-sister she had never met. She extended a hand, proud it did not tremble. "Deal."

Rumpelstiltskin produced a dagger of some dark metal Dahut did not recognise and drew a thin line along his palm, then proffered the blade to her. A moment, she stared at it. At the way the torchlight gleamed along the edge, vicious. She set the torch on the floor, took the blade. Drew a line along her palm, teeth gritted against the pain. Now, her hand trembled as she stretched it once more.

"Your birthright," the wizard said, holding out his palm. A single drop of blood spilled from it, splattering on the marble floor.

"My birthright for knowledge of how to find my baby sister," Dahut agreed. And she took his bloody hand in her own.

His long fingers closed around hers, squeezed, and he pulled her close. So close she could feel the warmth of his sickly-sweet breath on her face. She would never be queen now, had surrendered that to a sister she had never known. But she could find the missing babe. "The great ratna, that relic of the Celestials of Tianxia, brought hither by the fomorii and used to raise their great Tower of Glass, taken by Gofannon when the tower fell."

"The Celestial Jewel?" His grip had grown too tight. Dahut wanted to yank her hand away. She did not understand the whole of his words. "What of it?"

"Ask, and it shall show you all your heart desires, it shall, you, of the blood of Nudd." Abruptly, he released her, and Dahut stumbled backward, wringing out her hand.

When she looked up a moment later, Rumpelstiltskin had vanished from his throne. Dahut spun, whirling in the dark, casting about herself in dread. How had he moved thus? Still turning, still looking about, she knelt to retrieve the torch.

The whispering shadows loomed, monstrous in their dark expanses.

Heart hammering fast as ever, Dahut fled from the throne room.

ৡ

DAHUT WAS long in returning to Kêr-Ys. Winter was coming in, and with it came storms and the first snows, all of which reduced her homeward progress to a crawl. When she could, she rode with all the speed Morvoren could muster. For the longer she dawdled, the more peril to her infant sister.

That, and one other thing. One which she did not wish to admit. In her breast grew a sense of malaise, a disquiet that threatened to sway her from her course. That knot of apprehension had tightened with each passing day since she had left the Golden Mountain. But she could not afford to dwell on such, for she had staked her future on this task: the finding of a stolen babe. What matter that Dahut would never sit upon the throne, compared to the safety of her sister?

When at last she crossed through the gate and inside the sea wall, a dusting of snow blanketed the fields. The powder wasn't deep enough for children to build aught from it, which did not stop them from trying, dashing about and flinging handfuls at one another. At her too, as she rode by, for the children did not recognise their princess. The snow was not solid enough for a ball, so it merely sprayed over her mare as she passed, and she favoured the children with an indulgent smile.

And still, the unease quickened in her chest until she could no longer abide it. She kicked her mount into a canter and raced forward, toward the city. Barely, she resisted the urge to break into a full gallop. It called to her now, and she was so very, very close. Almost, she could feel the babe in her arms once more. Almost, she could see the girl's bright blue eyes or ruffle her flaxen hair. She would see the child named now, and would be there for her, all the days of her life. And one day, when their elder sister came for the throne, Dahut would be here to ensure the little one still had a life of ease and joy.

Such thoughts she focused on as she reached the city and was forced to slow Morvoren to a walk within the busy streets. As she made her way up the spiralling slope, toward the palace.

She handed her reins off to the stable hand, then raced through the halls of her home, almost breaking into a run. A sheen of sweat had turned her skin clammy, despite winter's chill. Not just exertion, but desperation, sending her heart pounding once again. The Vault of Ys lay beneath the palace, down several flights of stairs. The guards took note as she passed, for no one came there. Yet she was their princess, and she and her father alone had the keys to the vault, where the great treasures of the kingdom lay. There, they stored tributes of gold and silver from the many subject kings. Those, and more precious things—the masterful crafts of the Smith Lord lay within the vault.

But the most precious of all was the Celestial Jewel with which

Gofannon had wrought those works, even this very city. With it, he had worked wonders. With it, Dahut too would accomplish the impossible and retrieve her baby sister from the Sluagh who had stolen her.

At the base of the stairs, she came to the great stone door. Its surface was engraved with sinuous, serpentine dragons that wrapt around the frame and formed a border. Other than here, and within the vault, Dahut had never beheld such depictions of this sort of creature, and she had oft wondered where Gofannon had drawn his inspiration. But then, no one knew whence the Celestial Jewel had come, save Donn and Rumpelstiltskin had both mentioned Tianxia, perhaps some foreign land.

In the heart of the door was a great embedded lock. With tremulous fingers, Dahut withdrew the iron key from the chain around her neck. Why did this sense of dread come over her now? She had been in the vault before, on two occasions, and had felt only awe then. Now, her gut burbled in protest and her mouth had grown dry. The answers were right there, ready for her to claim them.

Her sister needed her.

Dahut slipped the key into the lock, turned it, shuddered as the mechanism clicked. Stone ground over stone, then a previously invisible seam opened in the middle of the door. Either side began to slide into the wall, revealing the chamber beyond. As the doors opened, hanging braziers flickered to life. Dahut knew they were fed whale oil via a thin channel threaded between their chains but had no idea how the mechanism worked. Like so much else built by the Smith Lord, the vault defied the logic of Man.

Around the chamber, in piles and chests, lay heaps of coin and mounds of gemstones. There were swords and spears hung upon the walls, and a statue clad in real mail and a gilded, gem-encrusted helm. There were strange tools on shelves, the usage of which her father had never been able to explain. None of those things mattered to her now, though. For in the centre of the room, in a circular depression, stood a sculpture of a dragon, like in form to those bedecking the door. It rose from its coils, bent back upon itself, but Dahut imagined, were Gofannon to have crafted it straight, it might have stretched ten or twelve feet long. As it was, it towered well over her head, its outstretched claw level with her eyes. Within that claw gleamed an opalescent pearl the size of her fist. The surface caught the firelight, absorbed it, bent it back until it seemed flames crackled in the heart of the jewel.

Ancient, distant gods had crafted this treasure and it had come to her line through the demigod Smith Lord, the source of all his wonders. So far as she knew, none of her line had ever tried to use it, not since the death of Gofannon. None had, heretofore, been rived by the sheer desperation that threatened to tear Dahut to pieces.

She reached for it, hand trembling. Her breath caught. This thing could tell her where her sister was. Indeed, if it could tell her that, what else might it answer? Could her family, had they known, have used it to avoid the murder of her mother and brother? But now she knew, and now she could make things right for all of them.

Her fingers closed around the pearl, soaked in its immense heat. A rush swept through her, a palpitation of her heart, a shudder of power akin to pleasure, the warmth of a bellyful of wine, of a caress along the back of her neck. She hefted the jewel. As she did so, a faint rumble ran through the palace. She had the impression the dragon statue had turned its gaze upon her, though it did not seem to have moved. Breathless, Dahut fell back several steps until her heel bumped the edge of the depression, a single step up.

The dragon stared at her. Its stony gaze scoured her, judged her for the temerity to try to use the Celestial Jewel. "I am of the blood of Gofannon," she rasped. "I am the whirlwind."

Another rumble set the room shaking, groaning. If she should be judged, then let her be judged; she would not abandon her sister. Never. "Show me the girl I seek, the sister Black Annis took from me." She stared into the fiery depths of that jewel, and it stared back. Phantasmagoric flickers took shape, perhaps inside the jewel, or perhaps in the eye of her mind.

Dark woods, dense upon mountainous slopes. Overgrown with foliage, the canopy letting in only sporadic bands of sunlight. Spruce and firs, blanketed in creeping moss. A tower amid the forest, vast and ancient, its foundations settling under the weight of time. Once, perhaps a watchtower in the far bounds of Nemedia. Was that ... the Black Forest? Images, ephemeral visions of the landscape around the tower. Enough, maybe, if she could consult those who knew the region ...

The Celestial Jewel had gone from warm to hot, stinging her palms.

Dahut blinked, tearing her gaze from its hypnotic depths. It seemed to bid her look back, look again. Look deeper and deeper until she would fall inside and be lost to the mortal world.

"Your birthright ..." A familiar voice said, from the shadows just beyond the mingled light from the braziers. "The great gift of Gofannon, left to his heirs ..." Of their own accord, Dahut's feet carried her up the step, toward the voice. The jewel cast its own faint luminance, pushing back the shadows, adumbrating the face of Rumpelstiltskin. The wizard reached out that emaciated, spindly limb of his, palm outstretched. "Your birthright, as promised ..."

Dahut's gaze darted to the jewel. "This? You ... you wanted the throne for my sister!"

"Your birthright." The wizard took a step toward her, swift, sure. His fingers curled into claws, like the grip of the dragon to which she must restore this jewel. "As you swore."

No. Dahut tried to speak the words, but her arm stretched out, against her will. She felt the oath she'd made settle upon her soul. Choice was torn from her. Teeth gritted with the strain, she tried to hold back the pearl, but still her hand reached for the wizard's. Turned, ready to drop the treasure into his waiting palm. "Don't do this ..." she pleaded.

"Your birthright."

The Celestial Jewel spilled from her hand into the wizard's. His fingers closed around it, a vise. His tongue darted out over his lips. "Ahh. This place, built with its power ... a shame, that."

Another quake, stronger, ripped through the chamber. Mortar cracked in the ceiling, sending showers of dust raining over her, and Dahut raised an arm to shield her eyes. When next she looked, Rumpelstiltskin was gone, vanished into the depths of shadows that ought not to have held him.

What had she done? For the second time, an Other had tricked her, cost her far more than she'd been prepared to pay for her aims.

Mammoth roars rumbled within the mountain, the entire city groaning in pain. The next tremor sent her stumbling, knees smacking down on the stone floor, sending bolts of lightning shooting through her legs.

Terror lent her the strength to cut through pain and she raced from the vault. All around her, the palace cracked at the seams. The walls bent, warped, protesting whatever was happening to them.

Dahut raced up the stairs, taking them two, three at a time, trying to escape the lower levels. She had to see what was unfolding above. She had to know ... Oh, gods what had she done! A colossal explosion sounded. The ground heaved, sending Dahut sprawling. Her head smacked on a stair.

She lay there, dazed. Hot blood trickled down her face, spilling over the steps, soaking her tunic. Words and thoughts fled from her, for a time. A block of masonry crashed into the stairs ahead of her, shattering them, drawing her from her stupor. Too scared—too hurt—to scream, instead, she managed a half run, half loping crawl.

The roar came then, and she knew. A rush of chaos and fury, like the reaching hand of the sea god Llŷr, come to reclaim land stolen from his domain. The sea wall had shattered, even as the whole of the city collapsed, and waves were rushing in, eager for space so long denied.

There was nowhere to go, nowhere to run. So Dahut ran nowhere. Just stood there, watching as the wall of water rushed down the hall, as it broke over her with such terrible force.

PART IV

When Gofannon, the son of Nemed, was grown, he crafted for his father a hand
of silver. Armed with argent limb, with his children at his side, Nemed returned
from the lands of Man to make war once again upon the Firbolg, who yet held
the better part of Inis Fáil. For demigod sons of Nemed could wield blades and
spears of wrought iron, accursed metal, against which the Firbolg could scarce
hold the ground. Thus did the Firbolg retreat from Inis Fáil, broken and bitter,
to found the last of the great cities, Falias, and forever after themselves be
known as the Sluagh.
>   —Annals of Findias, history of the Tylwyth Teg

4

———————

Though Donall had never promised me his heart, his choice now poisoned me with a venomous string of betrayal. Bitterness lanced my veins, colouring everything. The smoke of the hall stung my eyes. The music and laughter assaulted my ears with cruel violence. The joy of others rained over me in mockery of my anguish. Unable to bear it, I fled from Mael's hall and into the night. Once more, I found a thick fog had rolled in from the harbour, and this time, I welcomed it. For I lost myself in the brume, eager to vanish and never be found, least of all by my own treacherous heart. If this was love, why then did it cut so deeply? Everyone spoke of joy and warmth and companionship, but all I felt was that my longings had flensed and flayed me, leaving me to bleed out alone.

Faoinèis, I thought vicious. Donall, apathetic in his rejection—and somehow that was worse.

Such was my agony I expected to weep, but the tears would not come. I stumbled through the fog-drenched city, down toward the harbour, where the waters called to me. What a fool I had been! How could I have yearned for life in the surface world, when I knew so little of it? I had placed so much faith in Men, had thought, if I had once lived as one, I could do so again. Perhaps I ought to have considered my life in Kêr-Ys had ended in tragedy and destruction.

Cataclysm.

I reached the harbour and knelt upon a pier. Though autumn's bite had turned the sea frigid, I considered leaping off, imagining I could still swim home. As if I had not changed, as if what I had left behind would still await me. Oh, but some journeys could never be unmade. I knew it and *still* I thought of diving in and seeing how far I could make it, as if daring the sea to give back the parts of me I had callously cast aside. Now tears did spill from my eyes, the only part of me able to return to the sea.

I beat impotent fists against the pier, setting the boards to shuddering, but having no other effect. I had wrought my own doom, made my self-destructive choices, and all because I could not content myself with the life already before me. Now, as soon as Donall took the oath of his wedding, I would belong to the Kelpie. Had the spirit known all along how this must needs end? Aye, perhaps this was my punishment for stealing his prey. For now, my soul would take Donall's place, and I could blame no one save myself for that. I could not even curse the Kelpie, cruel as he was, for he had not tricked or compelled me down this path.

A long time I sat on the edge of the pier, ever imagining taking that plunge. Goosepimples prickled my flesh. Shivers ran through me, but I did not care enough to push myself up or seek out the warmth of the loathsome hall. By the Deep, I wanted to hate Donall for his choice, but I could not even do that. In his mind, Faoinèis had first saved his life and now offered him the chance to save his home through alliance. Who could fault him, then, for accepting a bond with her and becoming the hero he'd dreamt of being when he left to hunt for my sister?

Overhead, thunder rumbled, distant and wrathful. Dark clouds obscured the stars. Was that the Wild Hunt, riding out of Falias, seeking souls? If so, they remained distant, and I could summon no terror of them. Perhaps the Kelpie had already laid claim to the sum total of my fears. I did not know what would await my soul, but I knew enough to dread it.

"Lí Ban," a girl called from the water, and I turned toward a splashing. There, some distance off the pier, swam Mererid. Her beautiful ebony hair, once a mirror of my own, was gone, leaving her scalp glistening. My mouth hung agape to see her. Perhaps, even in the dark, her merrow eyes could see my missing tongue, for she gasped. "Oh, Lí Ban, it's true, then. What in the lightless depths of Naunet have you done to yourself?"

I spread my hands, as helpless to answer as I was to change my fate. At that moment, I threaded through self-loathing thick enough I could have drowned in it. My despair became a mire, and I wallowed in it, for it was the only sensation I could still feel.

I touched my head to ask over her hair, and she laughed without mirth. "I went to the Kelpie. I traded my hair for the chance to undo the change wrought in you." I wanted to ask how she had learnt I had gone to the ancient spirit, but I had no way to explain my questions, and Mererid seemed little inclined to elaborate. What pain I had caused her, as well! My heart ached over what I had done to my kin. I reached a hand toward her. She swam closer, then raised a hand. Not an empty hand, though, for she handed to me, hilt-first, a blade of rosy-gold metal. Was it orichalcum? Stuff of legend, a metal of Otherworldly power.

I took the knife, a question in my eyes.

"From the Kelpie," Mererid explained. "You must kill the man with it, then, at the shore, smear his blood across your legs. You can have your tail back, Lí Ban. If he dies before he makes the bond with another, your soul is *free*."

I stared, aghast, at the blade, then looked back to my sister. Kill Donall? How could I do such a thing? He had proved my truest friend. However he had hurt me now, I knew it had not come from a place of malice. Besides, I *loved* him. And now my life, my very soul would depend on my murdering him before he could wed another? The Kelpie's cruel sense of irony knew no bounds, it now seemed to me. This fresh torment was but one more punishment the spirit had conjured for me, completing his vengeance against me for stealing Donall from him. Mererid claimed she had gone to the Kelpie, but I suspected, rather, the spirit had lured her in, for it must have planned this all. His retribution was too perfect to have come about without a hand guiding it all.

No matter what I did now, the Kelpie won. Either I refused to slay my beloved and thus doomed my soul, or I destroyed that which I cherished most.

"You must do this," Mererid pleaded with me. Such sadness lurked in her eyes. "How can you hesitate to slay him? He is but a Man. Their lives are short, and besides, their best use is for filling our bellies." She was shaking her head, because she knew already I would demur. "Do not dither, Lí Ban. This is your only chance."

And had I not, moments before, longed to return to my home in Cantref Gwaelod? I could swim home tonight and take solace in the arms of my sisters, my father, my grandmother. I could flee all this and let it become a bitter memory of the greatest mistake of my life. Slowly, I stood and looked between the blade and my sister who had sacrificed her precious hair to procure it.

I could do it, I knew. I could get into his room, slay him, and escape in the night. There was no one to stop me from such a crime. No one, save myself. And I would prove the one foe I could never overcome, for I did not think I could live with myself having taken such a course. Did some remnant of the human life I had lived, surfacing in me, leave me incapable of the deed I knew any of my sisters would have done without hesitation?

"I'm sorry," I mouthed, and I hoped she understood. I knew how much she had paid for this, but I could not do it. Not this. The Kelpie would win and claim my soul. But at least it would prove the spirit who took that soul, rather than myself who destroyed it wilfully.

I let the blade tumble from my fingers. It splashed into the sea. A mournful look washed over Mererid and I knew she longed to weep but could not. Instead, I shed tears enough for the both of us, wracked by lachrymal convulsions that went on and on, as I slumped upon the pier. I wept until the seas ought to have risen from the flood of it. I wept until I had no tears left to shed.

In the end, my sister made no further attempt to sway me. Rather, she climbed a post of the pier until she could reach me, and wrapt me in her wet embrace. I scarce felt the chill, so glad was I of her arms. "Farewell, Lí Ban," she whispered into my ear. "You'll always be my favourite."

I kissed her brow. Then she dove back into the deep, and she was gone from me once more. Gone, like all I ever had.

I awaited the break of dawn, arms wrapt around my knees, shivering in the autumn chill. Even I knew better than to head outside the city in the night. Fae blood might have run through my veins, but it did not mean I would remain unmolested by the Tylwyth Teg, should they find me alone in the wild places. So I lingered, watching the sky for the spreading bruise that would herald sunrise.

Then it came, and still, I hesitated, for I could not believe it would end thus. I knew my time was short, and I could afford to waste none of it. I had, at best, a fortnight before the guests would arrive for the wedding. Once that day arrived, I was lost. Before that happened, I needed to find my stolen sister and see her to safety, wherever she was. Even so, the thought of leaving Donall felt akin to yanking an impaling blade from my flesh; it must happen, yet I knew it would only speed my death.

But what reason had I to linger now? So at last, with sunlight stinging my eyes, I made for the stables. I had ridden oft enough with Donall that I knew the process to saddle the animal. I slipped into the building and peered from one darkened stall to the next, hunting for Haggis. A hand fell on my shoulder, and if I could have screamed, I think I would have woken the whole of Bro Érech.

"What are you doing here?" a young voice demanded as I whirled on my accoster. It was the stable boy, his eyes widened with recognition on seeing my face. "You're the woman who came with Donall, aren't you?" I nodded. "You're taking her out for a ride so early, then?" Another nod. But he stared at me as if he saw something amiss. Guilt flushed my face, for I was, in fact, stealing my friend's horse. I hoped Donall would understand, though I could never explain. "Well," the boy said after a moment, "I was about to feed her. Best you wait until she's got some oats in her belly before going far."

The reminder set my own stomach rumbling, but I would not go back to the castle to break my fast. Still, I did not know much of land animals, and I could not risk harming the animal by taking her out without food, if this boy said otherwise. So I waited outside the stables, arms folded over my chest and watching my breath fog the morning air. Perhaps the locals would have thought me mad but seeing something like that still seemed almost magical to my eyes, and I never tired of it.

When enough time had passed I thought Haggis well fed, I trod inside and found the stable boy had wandered off to who knew where. Unwilling to wait a moment longer, I unlatched the gate and led the mare outside. There I came face-to-face with Donall, who watched me with uncertain eyes.

"My foundling?" he asked, his voice tremulous. "What is this?" Caught in the act, shame overcame me, and I glanced back between the mare and her owner. "You wanted to ride? I would have taken you, had you told me ..."

It struck me then that he had drawn so close to something he could no longer see its shape. He had spent so much time in my company and had never allowed himself to see the truth of my heart. And I was to blame for that, for I always thought I had more time, thought I could allow things to develop on their own course rather than risk them all before moving too fast. And now, in my melancholy and self-pity, I had intended to slip away without ever taking my leave. But how, after all our time together, could I do that to him? I owed it to him to be honest now. More, I owed to *myself* not to leave here without laying bare the truth.

My lip trembled as I placed my hands over my heart. *My heart is yours*, I wanted to say. One still on myself, the other I laid upon his breast. I felt both of our heartbeats, thumping in unison. We would have been a perfect match, save for a cruel twist of Fate.

His eyes widened and he staggered back, drawing a sharp breath. "F-foundling?"

Though I had adored his pet name for me, in that moment, it rained like blows on my ears and I longed for him to say my name. Just once, I wanted to hear him call for me. *Lí Ban, oh Lí Ban* ... But he never would, never could. My name would remain forever unknown to him. The irony was, in many ways, I felt he knew my soul better than anyone I had ever met. He had proved my truest friend, afore now. The pain in his eyes lanced me, the blade with which I had stabbed him having pierced us both. Unable to bear that look, I turned from him, taking the mare's reins and leading her away.

I managed a half dozen steps before a heavy hand seized my shoulder and spun me around. "Why didn't you say something sooner?" With a bitter snort, I opened my empty mouth at him. "Don't give me that!" His sudden outburst had me taking a step back. "You can make plain enough your meaning when you wish. As now, my foundling. So *why*?"

For the first time, he saw me; that, I could not deny. The realisation burned through me, painful as putting my hand in the fire pit, thrilling as those first steps on land when all was new and strange. I was floating with joy at the release of such a secret; my gut opened into a chasm of dread at how he would react, a fear so deep I could vanish into it and never again look upon the sky. My face was aflame, but my heart hammering, palms clammy. I was sweating all over, filthy with it.

Nor, could I deny his accusation. Indeed, my excuse was flimsy. *Because I was afraid*, I thought at him and spread my hands. *Because I imagined we had more time.* What a bitter irony, then, that mayhap things would have been different had I shown him this before we reached this city. Had I revealed my heart even a few days sooner, perhaps I would not now find myself drowning in this sense of loss. "I'm sorry," I mouthed at him, shaking my head.

Tears began to blur my vision. I was so, so sorry then, about everything. By the Deep, I had made so many mistakes. As Dahut, as Lí Ban, I saw my life as naught save a string of missteps, bringing tragedy to myself and those around me. Knowing he would back away, knowing it would only hurt more, I still reached for his face. And he did not withdraw, allowing me to cup his cheek. He clasped his hand over mine, and I felt his missing fingers. Oh, how I wanted to tell him everything! I wanted him to know the whole of me.

"You should have told me sooner." For certain. I knew my eyes would convey the depth of my regret. "If I break this engagement ..." I could not have heard that right. Did he truly consider leaving Faoinèis for me? Hope burgeoned in my chest, more frightening than the despair. With hope came once more something to lose. Maybe the worst fear is the fear of loss. His hand fell from mine, and sensing the change in his mood, I withdrew mine as well. "There will be consequences for this."

He rubbed a thumb along his brow. "Taranis's wrath, foundling. Why did you wait so long?"

Ire sparked in my heart then and I jabbed an accusing finger against his breast. *Should not you have known your own heart?* A second time I stabbed at him, then spread my hands, demanding an answer. For, if he chose me now, it meant some part of him had felt for me all along, but he had chosen to ignore that part of himself. If so, I would not suffer all the blame to land on my shoulders.

Donall hung his head, following my meaning. "Aye ... Well, no use dwelling on what either of us ought to have done, then, is there?" He pursed his lips and sputtered. "King Mael will not be pleased." Nor Faoinèis, I imagined. "Take Haggis to the harbour and wait for me by the ferry. I've a feeling we'll not be welcome guests in Mael's hall tonight."

A blush warmed my cheeks. All this ... was real? I could once more indulge in hope.

❦

BUT DONALL DID NOT COME and, as the morn waned, my worry swelled. What could have kept him in that palace after he had gone to call off the wedding? Could Mael have taken the rejection so ill that he would hold a guest as a prisoner? In the end, I decided I had no choice save to return. I led Haggis back to the stables, stroked her nose in reassurance, and let the stable boy take her to care for her.

I had set only a single step inside the palace vestibule when Faoinèis intercepted me, her face limned with fury. "I knew there was something wretched in you!" She wrung her hands, so vexed I half expected to see foam at the corners of her mouth. I stared at her, enduring her tirade, for in truth, we had wronged her. She had every right to that fury. "You are touched by the Otherworld."

Now *that* sent me falling back a step, shocked at her observation. Could all druids sense when something of Faerie drew nigh? Was she special? Reflexively, I glanced over my shoulder to make certain the way out remained unbarred behind me. I have no doubt Faoinèis took the guilty gesture for what it was.

The druid took a threatening step toward me, a predator closing in on her prey. "You have beguiled his senses with some enchantment."

A sad smile crept upon me at that, for had I not lost my voice, such a thing would have lain well within my power. But I had worked no arcana on Donall, and now I would not have done any such thing even if I could have. I had earned his regard all on my own, and Faoinèis could not stand the thought of it. I shook my head, though I knew she would never accept my denial.

The druid surged forward, seizing my hair and yanking my head back. "You will release him!"

My hands rose to fling her off, but something stayed me. I still did not know where they had kept Donall, and so it behoved me to play along with her for now, though allowing her to manhandle me chafed my pride. Still tugging my hair—my every instinct screamed for me to smash her to pieces—Faoinèis dragged me from the vestibule and into the main hall. There, Donall sat, expression dour as he stared at his sandals. A pair of men flanked him, both with spears, though neither had levelled the weapon. Still, their intent remained plain enough; Donall was indeed a prisoner of King Mael. Or of Princess Faoinèis, perhaps, as I think Mael would have taken Dùn Beinn by force with as much eagerness as he would by marriage.

"Release him from your spell, Other one," Faoinèis snarled at me, dragging me close to Donall.

My friend cocked his head to the side as if unable to believe the accusation the druid had hurled at me. "Foundling?"

Faoinèis shoved me toward my beloved, at last releasing my hair. "Break your hold on him!" Did she believe this, or had her heartbreak and desperation led her to convince herself the delusions she clung to were real? Despite it all, pity welled in me for the other woman. In her place, perhaps I would have thought the same things, told myself the same comforting lies.

The guards looked to me now, wary, the iron points of their spears rising. Perhaps they thought it unlikely a fae would wander into a city, but how could they know for certain? A touch of those blades would scald me, sure as fire. A thrust could end me. I lowered my gaze. I had no idea if I could move swiftly enough to overcome a trained warrior who already thought me a threat. This wasn't like that altercation in the market. In theory, my anáil allowed me to move faster and hit harder than a Man, but they were armed, and with *iron*.

But then, I could not allow harm to befall Donall or myself. If Faoinèis was desperate, I had grown more so. I lunged and seized the haft of one spear, yanking the startled guard aside. My strength sent him stumbling along the flagstones and crashing into a bench.

The other whirled his blade, not on me, but on Donall. "On your knees!" he roared.

Instead, I did the first thing that came to mind. I grabbed the rounded part of the spearhead and jerked it, wailing as the iron burnt the flesh from my palms. An acrid stench filled the hall as I wrestled the blade around, but I refused to let go. Faoinèis wrapt her arm around my throat and yanked me backward, but still I kept the spear point away from Donall.

He surged into motion, knocking the guard down. As the man tumbled to the floor, he released the spear, allowing me to let go as well. My palms had been reduced to raw, weeping ruins, blood oozing through charred cracks. Enraged and in pain, I jerked an elbow back into Faoinèis's ribs. A crack echoed through the hall the instant before her cries of agony filled the rafters. The woman dropped to her side, wailing.

Next I knew, Donall had my wrist and was yanking me after him, dashing back into the vestibule. He had no need to warn me more men would be coming. We ran for the harbour, our flight so frantic I almost managed to block out the pain raging in my hands. I'm sure neither of us wanted to leave Haggis behind, but we could not afford the least delay. In the harbour, Donall set his mind upon a small sailing boat, one laden with baskets full of fish. The boat's owner had begun to unload his catch. Donall ploughed into him, shoving him into the sea. "Sorry!"

I hopped into the vessel, and my beloved unwound the rope. Then I kicked us away from the pier. It sent the boat careening faster than I think Donall expected, and he slipped, caught himself on a rail, and mumbled some curse under his breath as he scrambled to the tiller. "It's true, though, isn't it? Epona preserve me, you're one of the Others."

Glowering, I held up my hands, palms out, so he could see the wounds I'd taken to save him. There was no denying my nature. Donall swallowed, but he did not recoil from me. "Well, even so. I've seen your heart, foundling. Such counts more than whence you hail." A moment, he was quiet, guiding us away from Bro Érech. "Aye," he said, when the city had grown small in the distance. "Aye, I'm with you ... but I think we're long overdue for a talk."

If only I had some way to give him all the answers he sought.

❧

HE RETURNED us to Mynydd y Gaer, across the strait, and there we took hospitality from King Dafydd, who was no particular friend of King Mael and, I think, still hoped Donall planned to save Rhys. That night we sat in Donall's room, staring at each other by the dwindling light of an oil lamp. Its waning flame sent shadows slithering around the chamber like octopus arms and cast most of my friend's face in darkness.

For a long time, he watched me. I sat with my back against the wall, crouched in a corner, cradling my throbbing hands against my belly as if I could block the pain thus. I can't imagine Donall could make out much more of my features than I could his, and perhaps less, for he was closer to the lamp and had but human eyes.

Twice, he grunted like he would speak and twice shut his mouth. Perhaps he feared the answers, though he knew he needed them. Much though I longed to tell him everything, I had no easy means to do so. Besides, I feared his reaction. He had not turned from me yet, but what if he came to believe the accusations Faoinèis had levelled at me? That I had bewitched his mind with Otherworldly power? Worse, what if he thought I intended to claim his life or his soul, as fae were wont to do?

"How did you come to me?" he ventured, at last. "How did you come to be washed up on the beach?" I thought for a moment, then pantomimed swimming. "Lost at sea? Aye, well, I gathered that much, but whence?"

From Cantref Gwaelod, but how did he expect me to provide a name? I pressed my feet together then kicked them side to side, in mimicry of how I would have swum with a tail. In the memory of Men, fomorii were ancient monsters of bygone times, rulers of the land, now banished beneath the sea. I had no idea how he would react on learning the truth, but I did not wish to keep it from him another moment. I needed him to know me, for good or ill.

He cocked his head, perhaps considering what I had said. But no, his gaze was higher, in the upper recesses of the room. I turned to look up at the corner. The shadows there swelled, a bloated umbral mass the dying lamplight could never account for.

Horrified, I scrambled away, closer to Donall, pulling the both of us to our feet. A spindly finger emerged from the dark, followed by others, fingers pulling a hand along like scrambling spider legs. A pale forearm followed, lurching oddly at the elbow.

"Teutates!" Donall cried, snatching the flickering lamp.

In the motion of the light source, I lost sight of the corner. Next I knew, something large plopped down onto the floor in a heap. As the lamplight washed over the creature, a fell, chittering laughter bubbled up from it. "Ooo, ahh. Hehe."

The being rose, looking for all the world a short, pale Man, limbs slender enough to look emaciated. The creature could have passed for mortal, but not to us, not after how it had appeared. Donall shifted the lamp closer, and I saw the cast of the fae's visage, and I drew a sharp breath.

For I knew this one, had seen him in my dreams. Rumpelstiltskin.

"Ooo," he chittered. "Remember me, do we, little Dahut? Heh. I do love a taste of irony, yes, I *do*. And this is the second time a princess has called me up to avenge a slight. Delicious, that."

I ought to have been terrified—I guess I was—but fury claimed me then. This creature had destroyed Kêr-Ys with his trickery and now stood before me. Though Donall tried to restrain me with an arm, I pushed forward, thrusting an accusing finger at the Sluagh. *Where is my sister?* I mentally screamed at him.

"Oh, the girl ..." he said, and I did not know if he had read my thoughts or just surmised my intent. "I do believe Gothel has her locked away in a tower. Hehe. That fruit ought to be just about ripe, now, eh? Now she's the older sister. But you ..." He sucked air between his teeth. "Succulent, to say the least, and only a cur without the least sense of poetry would settle for saying least." He held a hand to his mouth, then. "Oh, oops. Not saying much at all these days, you are, and a right shame. Mmm, mmm."

Where is the tower? I thought at him.

But if he heard my thoughts, he did not respond. Instead, he flowed closer, his spindly fingers closing around my wrist in a viselike grip. "First, you're bound for Falias, hmm. Then, me, I've got a payment to claim from another brash princess." The Sluagh licked his lips.

"You cannot have her!" Donall said, at last having recovered from the shock of seeing this creature enter our chamber thus. He surged forward, waving the lamp like a weapon. Something shifted beside me. An umbral tendril cracked like a whip and Donall staggered backward, then spilled onto his arse. Dazed, I saw him looking around, trying to see what had struck him. I caught but a glimpse—a welling of the gloom— then Rumpelstiltskin dragged me through the wall. The World shuddered. Colour bled out and everything turned to swirling greys and ultramarine shadows. For an instant, I could have sworn the buildings themselves contorted in agony. Then we were in the street outside the chief's hall, and Rumpelstiltskin was dragging me toward the harbour.

I tried to tug my wrist free, but the Sluagh was even stronger than I, and I would have sooner pried myself out of bronze manacles. "Poor, poor Dahut, twice over ill-fated. The stars have no love for you, no, no."

Desperate, I swung my free hand at his temple. He blocked the blow on his forearm and leant close. "Now, now, little merrow. Me, I find such violence crude, I do. Your kind and mine, Men drove us from this island, so I suppose we've a thing or two in common." He ticked his finger back and forth in my face. "What, so you think I ought not let them eat your soul? Hmm. The princess made a deal, she did, bade me drag you off to Falias. Hmm. Didn't bother to specify what I ought to do with you there. Might not be so bad ..."

He pulled me out, along the length of the pier, and set to untying a boat. "I mean, they could eat those new legs of yours, that's true. But I'm not opposed to another deal, once the taking of you there is done, Princess."

A feral scream reached me a moment before Donall came barrelling toward the pair of us, bared sword in hand. Rumpelstiltskin flinched from the iron blade, releasing me and sending me spilling to the dock. The Sluagh yanked a bronze dagger free from his belt. "If you sought death, you might've said so sooner and saved us both some trouble."

Donall closed in, swiping once more. Rumpelstiltskin ducked and kicked my beloved's leg out from under him. Before the Sluagh could drop down to impale Donall, I tackled Rumpelstiltskin, sending the both of us tumbling off the pier and into the dark, icy waters of the strait.

Everything was a blur of bubbles and murk and blackness. I flailed around, struck something solid—a post from the pier—and scrambled for air. Before I claimed it, something immense and sinuous wrapt itself around my waist and yanked me downward once more. The motion jerked me enough away from the pier that hints of silver moonlight illuminated the creature that had seized me: an eel, albeit one thick around as a person, wretchedly long.

It reared its head around and stared malice at me, beyond aught found in nature. For the Sluagh had taken this form. Its mass of muscle constricted around me, squeezing the air from my lungs. I fought, digging my nails into its slimy flesh and tearing rivets, but the pressure only increased. Rumpelstiltskin had bargained to take me to Falias ... did it matter if I was alive ... when ...

A splash, and then Donall was there, thrusting ineffectively with his sword at a giant eel head that danced away to either side with ease. It was going to kill him!

Flee, I screamed at him. *Save yourself!*

For I could do naught for him. Naught for myself, either, but the thought of him falling thus, it tore me apart inside. I wedged my fingers into the gouges I had made in the eel flesh and pulled, tearing skin down to sinew. Rumpelstiltskin convulsed, whirling on me with fresh rage, and those teeth flashed before my face but did not close. He wanted me alive.

Not Donall, though. And the Sluagh turned back to my beloved, and I knew I would lose him forever then. Because of me, Donall would die in the cold dark waters. A death not unlike the Kelpie would have given him, and all I had done was buy him time.

I turned a last, mournful gaze on the one person I wanted to save more than any other. I had failed him.

A surge of water rushed against us, and something collided with Rumpelstiltskin. Before my vision recovered, blood filled the water, and the Sluagh thrashed. The pressure on my insides was released, and I swam upward, bursting into the air and gasping for breath. The giant eel wriggled away beneath the surface, and I saw naught more of it.

Had Donall managed to strike it down after all? Was it possible a Man had saved me? He too burst above water and cast about himself as though bewildered.

Then another—bald—head rose from the waters, her appearance gentler as her gaze met mine. And my sister's arms were around me, carrying me to shore. Mererid swam by Donall, caught him up too, and eased us both to the beach beyond the ráth. There we lay, shivering, wracked by the cold and our injuries.

"Y-you're a fomor," Donall gasped, looking at Mererid, whose beautiful tail lay curled along the beach.

She looked to him and I could tell part of her wanted to blame him that I had not returned. "An old name, abandoned now. My sister and I are merrows."

He glanced back and forth betwixt her and me. "Sister."

"Aye, mortal. She is Princess Lí Ban of Cantref Gwaelod, though she surrendered that legacy for the chance to live in your world. And you will never know what else she gave up on your behalf, I think."

Donall took that in a moment before looking back to me. "But he ... that Other, he called you Dahut. Only, that was the name of the princess of Kêr-Ys. The one who died when the city fell." I nodded. "Your soul born again." Another nod. "That's why you sought with such fervour after the lost princess. She's your sister." He fell silent a moment. "That one, he named the one who took her, called her Gothel. It's a clue we did not have before."

It was, and I only now, with the immediate threat past, could begin to think on what it meant. With a name, perhaps we could find the Sluagh and her tower. At last, maybe we could find my sister.

But my *other* sister had saved us, and now I crawled to her and flung my arms around Mererid and wept into her shoulder. She held me, humming softly, without speaking. I knew better than most: sometimes words were not needful.

જ

Donall told me that, whilst he convalesced at the Fane of Teutates, a knight of Ys had come in search of my sister. This I recalled, too—I had given Sétanta the task of finding the babe. I had never imagined he would still search for her, seventeen winters later. More of my memories of that past life had continued to surface, pieces of my time as Dahut, coming to me in dreams, in fitful visions, in sudden realisations.

War would surely come now, betwixt Bro Érech and the clans of eastern Inis Fáil, Donall's kin included. Mael would move against them, but not until spring, and it gave us a few scant, treacherous months to find sign of my sister. It meant, though Donall asked me to wed him and I had agreed—a thing I once never could have imagined—time did not favour us.

So Donall sought out Sétanta and we met him along the banks of the Renos, outside a small town. Across the water, I could see the dense woods of the Black Forest. Tale claimed several duchies lay within, all but cut off from the outside by the encroaching foliage. Once, those lands too had been part of Nemedia but broke away when Owain, a son of Nemed, vanished.

The surface world was vast and wild, and Men, I learnt, controlled but small enclaves in that immensity. If Gothel had taken my sister into the wilderness, we might search for a century and not find the least sign of her. But Rumpelstiltskin had told us my sister dwelt in a tower, which was a place to start as we hunted a particular drop of water in the ocean. I knew, too, that tower had to be in a forest, for I had such memories, from the Celestial Jewel, as Dahut. As woods covered so much of the uncultivated lands of Golgleth, that helped but little.

Our journeys were not without difficulty. Donall had only a handful of coins remaining, and we now stretched them, foraging what food we could. Sometimes he hunted or fished, and I watched, a tad bitter I could no longer simply chase down a fish and snatch it with my bare hands. Life among Men had its hardships. As did life as a human woman, I soon learnt, when my body underwent a horrid process of cramps and blood loss. Donall assured me it was both natural and recurring—how pleasing that was to learn!—but the man seemed so uncomfortable to speak of it, I feared to push him for more answers. It seemed I had not had the least idea of just how unknown a world I entered when I bargained with the Kelpie.

Sometimes, I asked myself whether, knowing all I knew now, I would make the same choices. The question tugged at me, for part of my soul must always long for that palace of amber, beneath the sea. I would forever wake, yearning to hear the voices of sisters gone from me. Once, I felt trapped by the world beneath the waves; now, I missed the freedom I had to swim wherever I wished. Would I make the same choice again?

I think that I would.

At night, I lay in Donall's arms, warm and safe and loved. Day by day, as he improved at intuiting my thoughts, he answered all my thousand, thousand questions about Mankind and the surface world. I had lost something precious, but I had gained something worth even more.

On the cusp of winter, Sétanta rode toward us on a roan and I felt an instant pang of loss for Haggis, as I'm certain did Donall. Leaving her behind meant losing a friend. The knight dismounted, and now, seeing him up close, I realised time had weathered the boy I had known in Kêr-Ys. But of course it had. Years of hard searching, of failure, and of whatever vices proved needful for him to continue in spite of that failure, they took their toll. Time had no mercy.

"Donall," Sétanta said, clasping my beloved's arm. "They say you bring word of the lost princess."

"Some." Donall released him and motioned for the man to join us where we had made a rough camp. A small fire crackled, pushing back the chill. Already, I had seen flurries of snow yester morn. The thought of seeing the world blanketed in white had my heart soaring, though I knew Donall did not share my enthusiasm, always bemoaning how hard it would make travel. He claimed we would freeze in our boots, our toes numb, and repined over the time we would lose, holed up to wait out storms. I could scare wait for it.

The knight plopped down in a huff, then scratched at what looked like a fortnight's worth of stubble. Whatever care he'd taken for his appearance in his youth, all had fallen by the wayside now. His clothes were mud spattered, his hair dishevelled. Dark shadows welled beneath his bloodshot eyes. "Tell me."

"We learnt the name of the one who took her." Donall tossed the knight a skin of wine. Such was in short supply, but Sétanta seemed to need it more than we did. "It was Gothel. According to what we heard, she has her locked in a tower in a forest."

"Doesn't much narrow the search." The knight uncapped the skin and took a long swig before handing it back. "Woods are everywhere. Can you tell me which kingdom?"

Donall shifted. "We think the Black Forest, but we don't know it for a certainty. But at least you know she lives. And with a name for her abductor ..." He hesitated. "I've word of her sister, too."

"What, the princess Dahut?" Sétanta grimaced, looked away. "She's dead."

"Aye, and born again." He cocked his head in my direction.

His gaze settled on me, brow raised. After a moment the man snorted. "I'm expected to believe that? Tell me you didn't drag me out here for this absurdity. Is this some sort of angling for the throne of High King, what, to claim you've wed the reincarnated daughter of Gralon, now?"

"I'm not seeking the throne. Even were I ..." Donall held up his maimed hand, for law held no man who was not whole could be king.

Sétanta's regard returned to me, heavy as a blow. "And you? Have you aught to say for yourself, then, *Princess*?"

"She cannot speak."

"Oh, convenient."

I crawled over beside him and laid a hand on his cheek, as I had once done as Dahut. The knight stiffened a moment, then recoiled, perhaps placing the gesture in his memory and rejecting it as impossible. "What in Esus's arse is this?"

"Dahut sent you to find her sister," Donall said.

Now the knight's eyes darted back and forth between myself and my beloved. "You ... might have heard that from someone."

I signalled to Donall, using the private language of hand gestures we had begun to develop between us. It was no substitute for words, not yet, but it allowed me to convey meaning well enough. Donall's face darkened, displeased, and indeed, I had not wanted to tell him what I now shared. "She says ... she bestowed on you a kiss. Once ..." He looked at me, sullen. "Maybe more than one. Lí Ban ..."

I rolled my eyes. Was he to take umbrage over what I had done in another life? Such petty jealousy did not become him, and he well knew it.

Sétanta fell silent, withdrew into himself a time, staring not so much at me as out into the middle distance behind me. I gave him time. It must have been a hefty weight dropped on him. The only sound was the crackle and pop of the fire. "How can you know that?" he asked after the quiet had dragged on rather too long. "You cannot know *that*."

I cocked my head to the side and offered a sad smile. In a life that had never materialised, I had imagined something between him and me, and perhaps he had too. Like my life in Cantref Gwaelod, that life too had vanished forever, existing only in memory. In dream.

"It's true then ...?" The knight swallowed and swept his hair from his face. "Gods! Dahut? Is that ... can it be?" He reached toward me, but Donall cleared his throat.

"She's Lí Ban now and betrothed to me."

Sétanta's hand dropped down to his thigh. "Why tell me this?"

"Because you're sworn to find her sister. For so many years, you searched alone, but you have allies now. Together we can—"

"There's no together."

I stiffened, and Donall shifted. "What?"

"Are you a knight? Is *she*? The wilds are thick with beasts. Worse, with the Others and perils you cannot fathom. Me, I'm a lone wolf, and I hunt alone. You know what they call me, in the Black Forest? The fen-dweller, Fenrir, the say. You want the princess found, keep doing as you have, feeding me information. Leave the trackless expanses to me."

"But—"

"Word on the wind claims war heads toward your lands. And what, you think you can avert it this way? You think you find the lost princess, Mael will accept that and stand down? Such are the self-delusions of children. Go home, Donall, and prepare your people for war. Seek what allies you can find."

But Donall had failed to recover the souls from the Kelpie. Samhain had come and gone, and many of the chiefs would not look kindly upon him for having made a promise he could not uphold. Still, would they side with us against an invader from the continent? They might. Though it stung, I knew Sétanta had the right of this. We would prove little boon in searching the woodlands, and we might well lose Donall's home in the process.

I laid a hand on Donall's knee and nodded.

SÉTANTA LEFT IN THE MORN, and I embraced him. For once, we had been close, and now my hopes rode with him. Donall and I took a ship back to Inis Fáil. Winter weather made the crossing perilous, and I was struck by the oddity of fearing being tossed into the sea. Such fear made the voyage somewhat surreal.

We returned to Dùn Beinn and informed Donall's father of all that had passed. Donall did not tell him of my past life—we agreed to share that with no one else—and I do not think the man much approved of his son taking a mute foundling as a bride. He did not approve, but he loved his boy and he made no move to interfere.

Men set about the forges, crafting weapons, while others trained with spear or blade or sling. Riders were sent, despite the storms, to other ráths, seeking alliance against Bro Érech. The winter passed all too swiftly, and we could only hope we were ready. Some other chiefs had agreed to side with us. Some, but perhaps not enough.

Our hopes, in the long run, despite Sétanta's words, may have still lain with my lost sister, and with the last loyal Ysian knight who sought for her.

Just before the spring festival of imbolc, I wedded Donall. I could not speak the oath, could only bow my head in acknowledgment. Donall placed a ring of carved pearl on my finger, though I've no idea how he acquired such a thing.

Nor did I know what the future would hold.

Only one thing I knew: we would face it together, my husband and I.

EPILOGUE

*R*umpelstiltskin stepped from the shadows of the mountain pass and out onto the plateau where the Golden Castle sat, an etiolated monument to bygone days. The foundations had settled, cracks spread through the walls, and gaps where blocks had crumbled let in the chill draughts of winter. In his palm he held the Celestial Jewel, and he glanced down at the pearl. So easy to imagine himself restoring this place to its former glory. With this in hand, he could craft works equal to the Smith Lord, and perhaps he would.

Perhaps this place would become a new capital for a new empire. He had not expected Kêr-Ys to crumble as it had, had not known that the power of the jewel alone kept the walls standing. No, but perhaps he should have. Well, it mattered little in the end. His girl, his beautiful girl, she would have her own birthright now. Nudd's blighted blood was spent, worn thin. Dahut must surely have perished, and the babe Gothel had taken would claim no throne, he knew.

Here, in his daughter's name, Rumpelstiltskin would build a new Nemedia, one to rival even the works of Falias, or any of the cities of Dark Faerie. His brethren would be forced to bow, to subjugate themselves before him and his girl, and she would reign over them, fierce and beautiful. One day ... one day, a dark queen.

He made his way within his castle, trying not to dwell on how he'd come to this place, more site of exile than of reward. Dead, dead, so many, and him alone for so long, before his girl came. Now, for her he had reason to live, to plan, to scheme once again, as in days gone.

Still staring at the jewel, he ascended the stairs but started on the landing, for Blodeuwedd stood there in her night shift, looking at him. She was a woman grown now, really, and soon she would be ready for her birthright. At the moment, though, he saw a barefoot, freezing lass in need of a pillow and a warm blanket. "Father? You found what you were seeking?"

Rumpelstiltskin shifted his gaze from the jewel to his daughter and back. She stood there, fidgeting with the flax straw he kept around to spin to gold. Always fidgeting with it, so nervous. "I found it. It's late, though, and you ought to be well abed. Sleep now, my beauty, and we'll talk when you've rested." When he, too, had rested, for the journey had taken somewhat out of him, and he could do with a while to muse on things. Ages passing left one accustomed to time with one's thoughts until all other voices seemed distant. Sometimes, the elders, they forgot ... everything, outside themselves, wandering solipsistic pathways, lost in mazes of their own minds.

"The dreams ..." she said. Her pensive voice snapped his gaze to her face.

He advanced, laid a hand upon hers where it rested upon the balustrade. "Again?"

She looked away, staring down into the gaps in the walls, where the wind howled like a feral wolf. "Always."

"There's power in dreams, beauty. You need not fear them." Except when fear proved needful. But to say such would little help her. "Sleep, darling. I'll be at hand to hold back the nightmares, promise."

After a last shiver, his daughter nodded and plodded down the hall, to her chamber. Dahut had looked rather like Blodeuwedd, he mused, not for the first time. The same dark hair, the same facial structure. Well, she was doubtless dead now, after the cataclysm that swallowed Kêr-Ys, and Rumpelstiltskin would not grieve her, blood of Nudd. He clucked his tongue, not wanting to work himself up, dwelling on hoary resentments toward one long dead.

No, no. No time for that sort of indulgence. Not for him, the peril of memory. Resolved, he made his way down to his desolate throne room, vast and empty, as if in mockery of things lost. They did not matter now, not now he had his beauty, his girl.

With a huff, he collapsed in a heap upon his golden throne and kicked a leg over the armrest, admiring the burning jewel in his palm. A Celestial Jewel, like unto the one that blazed in the heart of Falias, in the hearts of all the cities of Dark Faerie. Handed down from the days of the Celestials, and so few remained to power the crafting of wonders.

Well, when he was done, Blodeuwedd would sit upon a throne above all the lands, and even dread Gwyn would hesitate to cross her. They all would, that was the legacy he would give his child.

A long time, he stared into that jewel, and it whispered to him of secrets and of powers it could bestow. Of designs grand, of majesty not yet lost to this world, despite its slow slide into the maw of entropy.

He did not hear the other enter his throne room, only noted her when Gothel stood a dozen feet ahead of him. "You *betrayed* me!" the woman spat at him. "You revealed me, my spire to Men. To the blood of Nudd."

Rumpelstiltskin shrugged. "Dead now. What care have you what the dead know or do not know, Sister?"

She held up a hand. "You lost the right to call me that long back. And now *this*, what, to taunt me?"

"A jest," he lied, for providing the answer about Gothel had given him the needful means to manipulate Dahut and thus gain her birthright. "I knew she would not live to act upon her accursed knowledge." Another lie.

"A jest?" Gothel asked, seeming to ponder that a moment. "Only a jest. Though you know I need the blood of Nudd. Still just a jest?" She spread her hands. "Well, allow me to *jest* in turn, *Brother*. In the name of our common blood, I lay my curse on yours." His stomach dropped at the sudden realisation of his peril, and he lurched from his throne, but it was already too late, she was already speaking. "That your girl shall prick her finger on a seed of flax straw and sleep eternal."

"No!" Rumpelstiltskin surged for his sister, but Gothel fell back, retreating into the shadows. He could have pursued, but what would it avail him? Words spoken flew like arrows from a bow. No taking them back, never back.

Instead, he ran from the throne room, a mad dash for her chambers.

Stumbling, tripping over his own feet in his haste, shoulder slamming into the corner. He hardly felt the impact. "Blodeuwedd!" he bellowed. "Blodeuwedd, don't touch aught! Beauty, answer me! My beauty!"

He crashed in through the door to her rooms and, finding her not in the antechamber, raced inward, to her bedroom. His daughter lay sprawled on the floor, a piece of the flax straw still clutched in her hand. Rumpelstiltskin choked on an outburst of grief, on denial this was even possible. He collapsed beside the girl, laid his ear upon her chest.

Her heart yet beat, but slowly, a sleep too deep. Far too deep.

"No, no, no." He cradled her head in his lap. "Blodeuwedd ... My beauty ... Blodeuwedd?"

Time and again he tried to wake her, knowing it impossible. For Gothel's curse was strong, born of her pain, born of the common bound they shared. And now, now *his* pain was strong. "I won't let her profit from this," he promised Blodeuwedd. "Her girl shall be taken from her. That ... Rapunzel of hers." He sucked down ragged breaths, holding back his weeping. "Ooo, I'll let her come *almost* of age, almost to where she needs her. And then she'll see how it feels to lose on the cusp of victory." He stroked his daughter's dark hair and gently hefted her in his arms, carried her to her bed. "I promise, my beauty. I promise. This is not over."

Join the Skalds' Tribe newsletter and get access to exclusive insider information and a selection of free books to kickstart your Matt Larkin library.

https://www.mattlarkinbooks.com/skalds/

ALSO BY MATT LARKIN

Gods of the Ragnarok Era

The Apples of Idunn

The Mists of Niflheim

The Shores of Vanaheim

The High Seat of Asgard

The Well of Mimir

The Radiance of Alfheim

The Shadows of Svartalfheim

The Gates of Hel

The Fires of Muspelheim

Tapestry of Fate

The Gifts of Pandora

The Valor of Perseus

The Inferno of Prometheus

The Madness of Herakles

The Threads of Theseus

The Face of Hekate

The Wrath of Artemis

The Circle of Kirke

Heirs of Mana

Tides of Mana

Flames of Mana

Queens of Mana

For my Juhi and Kiran.

Special thanks to my family and my team that helps bring these projects to life:
Sarah, Regina, Nada, and Francesca.

www.ingramcontent.com/pod-product-compliance
Lightning Source LLC
Chambersburg PA
CBHW030827200726
48285CB00007B/2381